"Please, _____
*her voice soft as a baby's breath,
pleading with him. "I want..."
she said breathlessly. "I need..."*

"What?" His own voice was thick and husky. "What do you want, Dodie?"

Not chocolate, Dodie thought.

He lifted his head, caught her lower lip between his teeth and grazed it gently, teasing it with the tip of his tongue, tasting her. "You're beautiful, Dodie," he said.

"Beautiful?" He heard the soft choked sound as, painfully, she tried to laugh. "Please...."

"Beautiful," he insisted. "Don't let anyone ever tell you otherwise."

WHAT WOMEN WANT!

It could happen to you...

Every woman has dreams—deep desires, all-consuming passions, or maybe just little everyday wishes! In this brand-new miniseries from Harlequin Romance® we're delighted to present a series of fresh, lively and compelling stories by some of our most popular authors—all exploring the truth about what women *really* want.

Step into each heroine's shoes as we get up close and personal with her most cherished dreams...big *and* small!

- Is she a high-flying executive...but all she wants is a baby?
- Has she met her ideal man—if only he wasn't her new boss...
- Is she about to marry, but is secretly in love with someone else?
- Or does she simply long to be slimmer, more glamorous, with a whole new wardrobe!

Whatever she wants, each heroine finds happiness on her own terms—and unexpected romance along the way. And she's about to discover whether Mr. Right is the answer to her dreams—or if he has a few questions of his own!

This month enjoy *The Bridesmaid's Reward*
by Liz Fielding.

Next month, look out for *Surrender to a Playboy*
by Renee Roszel, #3752.

THE BRIDESMAID'S REWARD

Liz Fielding

HARLEQUIN®

TORONTO • NEW YORK • LONDON
AMSTERDAM • PARIS • SYDNEY • HAMBURG
STOCKHOLM • ATHENS • TOKYO • MILAN • MADRID
PRAGUE • WARSAW • BUDAPEST • AUCKLAND

ISBN 0-373-03749-X

THE BRIDESMAID'S REWARD

First North American Publication 2003.

Copyright © 2002 by Liz Fielding.

This edition published by arrangement with Harlequin Books S.A.

CHAPTER ONE

'DODIE? What's happened? Calm down! Deep breath...'

Dodie Layton, having bombarded her best friend with an almost incoherent appeal for help, took a long, slow breath, as ordered, but her heart continued to race and her legs remained nothing but jelly.

'Okay now?'

She nodded, although since this was a telephone call Gina wouldn't be able to see her.

Gina knew her well enough to fill in the gaps, however, and said, 'Good. Now, tell me all that again. Slowly.'

'I've got six weeks to lose two dress sizes and transform myself from Miss Blobby into Bridesmaid of the Year,' she said, editing her first garbled rush of information to its essentials.

'You are not a blob. You're...'

'Cuddly?' Dodie offered while her best friend gamely sought for a kindly euphemism to cover her generous curves, the width of her bottom, thighs that gave cellulite a bad name. 'That is not a comfort. My sister—the thin, beautiful, young one—'

'You've only got one sister.'

'—the one who's been nominated for every film award going in the last twelve months. Star of stage, screen and telly. Loved by everyone—'

'Listen, I *know* your sister. I remember her when she had zits and braces on her teeth—'

'—is getting married.' Gina, silenced by this stunning piece of gossip, gave her the opportunity to cut to the chase. 'And I've been cast as chief bridesmaid,' she finished.

'Oh, wow!'

'Oh, disaster!' Dodie wailed, reaching for the toast she'd been buttering when her mother rang with the big news. Along with strict instructions to reduce her dress size pronto and a promise to put details of the very latest diet—guaranteed to work practically overnight—in the post. Since she was far too busy to bring it over. Obviously.

Dodie tucked the telephone beneath her ear while she sloshed on an extra thick layer of marmalade before taking a bite. She'd cut down on the calories later; right now she needed sugar for the shock.

'I don't suppose I need to ask who she's marrying?' Gina asked, her attention now fully focused on the really important matter of hot gossip. 'The diary columnists have been salivating for weeks over rumours that the on-screen lovers were doing it for real. When's the big day?'

'I can't tell you the exact date. It's a state secret, apparently, but early May seems to be favourite.' She groaned again. 'I've got six weeks, Gina. I need to jog. I need weights. I need aerobics,' she said, spluttering toast crumbs everywhere as she wondered what had happened to all those resolutions she'd made on New Year's Day. 'I've got to do all those things I've been putting off for ever and—'

'What you've got to do is stop talking with your mouth full and get a grip.'

'Right,' she said. She wasn't about to disagree with the only person in the world who could get her into shape in time. She swallowed the toast. 'I can do this,' she said firmly. 'In fact my heart's beating so fast with the excitement that I'm losing calories just talking to you.'

'I'm sorry to disillusion you, but for any loss of weight the raised heartbeat needs to be the result of exercise.'

'Really?'

'Really.'

'Oh, well, you know more about this than I do. Which is where you come in.'

'Oh, right. All becomes clear.'

'Look, do you want to come to this wedding or not?' Dodie demanded, stooping to outright bribery. 'The guest list is going to be a *Who's Who* of the film and theatre world. Actor knights. Pop stars. Starlets in wildly unsuitable dresses hoping to make the front page—'

'Why would your sister ask me to her wedding?'

'I get to ask someone. As in "and partner".'

'Er, isn't that supposed to be a bloke?'

'That's a very un-PC comment, Gina,' she said primly. 'This is a showbiz wedding. And anyway, I haven't got a bloke.' She was planning to keep it that way. 'Besides, I wouldn't want a man along cramping my style. I mean, isn't the chief bridesmaid supposed to arouse feelings of unrestrained lust in the best man? Traditionally?'

'I'd heard that rumour, although personally I've

never seen one worth getting excited about.' Dodie didn't say anything. 'Oh, *right*. I think I'm beginning to understand the unlikely attraction of wearing some hideous satin, frill-covered concoction. And why you're even considering getting toned up for the occasion. Come on, give. Who is it?'

'The best man, do you mean?' she asked casually, as if this wasn't the reason her heart was quivering like a greyhound in the slips, throbbing like a Ferrari in pole position at Monaco, pounding like…like the entire drum section of the Royal Marine band at the Edinburgh Tattoo. And for a moment she had to grip the back of a handy chair—this kind of excitement was really too much to deal with over breakfast. 'The best man is going to be Charles Gray.'

Being human, she took a certain amount of pleasure in the resulting stunned silence that positively vibrated down the telephone line.

'Charles Gray?' Gina responded finally, with gratifying awe. 'Heartthrob and sex god? The man every right-thinking woman wants to find under her tree on Christmas morning wearing nothing but a smile and a condom? *That* Charles Gray?'

'Yes. Total fantasy.' And she sighed. 'Absolutely perfect, in fact. One day of enchantment without any messy long-term reality to ruin the effect.'

'You plan on turning back into a pumpkin at twelve o'clock?'

'On the dot. And I'll be a lot more careful with my shoes than Cinderella. I mean, let's be honest, what are the chances that she lived happily ever after with a man fixated on her feet?'

'I'd never given it any thought,' Gina admitted.

'And of course your eagerness for me to wave my magic wand and turn you into a princess for the day has absolutely nothing to do with the fact that Martin will see the pictures in *Celebrity* magazine and realise that he could have been there, rubbing shoulders with the rich and famous? Imagine the caption… *Mr Martin Jackson, partner of the bride's lovely sister, Miss Dodie Layton, chatting to composer and well-known art collector, Sir Thingummy Whatsit…*'

Reminding her about Martin didn't have quite the effect Gina would have wished. Far from being amused, Dodie was only reminded just how undesirable she was. Casting a hopeless look down at herself in her working clothes—barrage balloon jogging pants that had never been jogged and a T-shirt that appeared to have shrunk in the wash—she groaned.

'I'm just fooling myself, aren't I? It'll never happen. I'm going to look like a lumpen fool amongst all those toned, tanned and skinny celebs. As out of place as a lily on dung heap, in fact.' As the reality of the situation sank in she broke off and grabbed another slice of toast. 'Charles Gray being the lily.'

'Nonsense,' Gina said, with gym mistress briskness. 'Don't put yourself down.' Okay, so she wasn't a gym mistress, she was the manager of a seriously upmarket health club at the newly opened Lake Spa complex, but she could give a good impression of one when she was feeling bossy. 'He couldn't have a more charming companion at a wedding. You're every bit as pretty as your sister. This may be considered heresy in some circles, but I think her cheekbones are a bit, well, bony. Contrary to popular myth, it is possible to be too thin.'

'The camera loves bone.'

'Maybe, but you're not an actress, and, with or without bone, your smile would light up any occasion.'

Gina meant to be kind, she knew, but that was exactly the reaction Dodie most dreaded. It wouldn't be so bad if she didn't constantly have to stand comparison with her incredibly beautiful, incredibly talented, incredibly *thin* sister. But, having cast about for something complimentary to say, desperate relatives who hadn't seen her for a while always plumped for the safety of her ''lovely smile''.

Well, this time it wouldn't be enough.

'Since my ''lovely smile'' will have to compete with that of the terminally sexy Mr Gray's, I doubt it will make much impression. I'll just be that girl wearing a frilly tent and grinning inanely in all the photographs.' And, groaning again, she abandoned the astringency of the marmalade and opened the fridge door. There was a jar of chocolate spread tucked away at the back that she kept for emergencies such as this.

'I didn't mean it about the frills, Dodie. Your sister has far too much good taste to put adult bridesmaids in frills.'

'Maybe the frills are metaphorical, Gina, but the sniggers will not be—unless you, my dearest, oldest friend, save me from myself. I need the kind of one-on-one help that only someone who's shared your most intimate secrets since nursery school, who knows your every weakness, can give. Who else would know where I hide the secret supplies of chocolate? Those biscuits I keep for the really bad moments? My addiction to soft, melting Camembert piled onto a Bath Oliver—?'

'Stop it right now!'

'I'm a hopeless case,' she said. 'In moments of stress you go for a run. I just reach for food. My mother only had to mention the words ''instant miracle diet'' for me to break out in a sweat. I'm on my knees here, begging you to move in with me for the duration, keep me on the straight and narrow—'

'I'd do anything for you, Dodie, you know I would, but—'

'But? Don't tell me ''but'', Gina. I can't handle ''but''…'

'But,' she said, ignoring the rising panic in Dodie's voice, 'our friendship has always been on a live-and-let-live basis. I've tolerated your love affair with the diet from hell. You've tolerated my need for the endorphin high of exercise. Ours is a relationship based on mutual respect for our individual no-go areas and I think we should leave it that way. And,' she went on before Dodie could interrupt, 'even if I wanted to help I couldn't. I was just about to call you and ask if there was anything in Los Angeles that would make your life truly wonderful.'

'Los Angeles?'

'My company is sending me to the US to check out the latest trends in the health and leisure club scene over there. I leave today.'

'You're kidding!' Dodie forgot her own problems for a moment, excited for her friend. 'That's fantastic.'

'I do feel a bit as if I've stepped into a fairytale myself,' Gina agreed. 'I was given *carte blanche* to choose my own team at the health club. And now this. My degree in business management has finally connected with my real life and I'm going places.'

'Los Angeles, apparently. That's such good news, Gina. I'm so pleased for you.' Then, 'I just wish you were going places some other time. Couldn't you put it off for a couple of months?'

'Not even for you, sweetheart. But I'll offer some sound advice. Ignore your mother's "instant" diet. There is no such thing.'

'But—'

'I mean it. The answer is to cut out the bad stuff— and you know what that is without me telling you— and get some exercise. What I *can* do,' she said, cutting off Dodie's wail of anguish, 'is sort you out a personal trainer. Someone to put together a pro- gramme for you and keep you at it.'

Some stranger who wouldn't know all her little foibles?

'I'll backslide without constant help,' Dodie said. 'Right now, for instance, I'm taking a pot of choc- olate spread out of the fridge.' She'd finally found it lurking in the depths of the salad bin, where she'd tucked it away out of temptation. Sadly, all that re- mained was a slick of chocolate clinging to the sides of the jar. But Gina didn't know that. 'I'm going to spread it half an inch deep on this really thick slice of toast,' she said, fingers crossed as she stretched the truth until it twanged. She did have the toast, however, and, holding it close to the phone, she took a crunchy bite. 'It's white bread,' she warned, mumbling through a mouthful of crumbs.

Gina just laughed. 'Nice try, Dodie, but it'll take more than that to stop me from catching my flight. Look, why don't you forget the diet, relax and just enjoy yourself at the wedding? Wear something low-cut and the starlets won't get a look in with the photographers, believe me. Besides, Charles Gray is probably bored to death with girls who are little more than skin and bone.'

'Are you supposed to say things like that? It's your business to get women down to skin and bone.'

'It's my business to get them fit. There's a big difference. Besides, it'll probably be a whole new experience for him to dance with a woman-sized woman. An armful of cuddle. A bit of a treat, in fact.'

'Get real.'

Gina sighed. 'Martin Jackson didn't cheat on you because you were a few pounds overweight, Dodie. He did it because he's a Class A piece of—'

Dodie took another crunchy bite of toast to drown out the word Gina used. She knew what Martin was. It didn't make what he'd done—or the fact that he'd done it with a girl the size of a stick insect—any easier to bear.

'I'm more than a few pounds overweight now.'

Gina kindly refrained from pointing out that she'd done that to herself. Instead she went straight to the point, the way she always did.

'What do you really want, Dodie?' she asked.

'I want to be thin, I want to be beautiful, I want

heads to turn wherever I go.' Like her sister. If she was going to dream, she might as well dream big.

After a momentary pause—probably to pick herself up off the floor—Gina said, 'Oka-a-a-y. Let's start with the weight—get that right and everything else will fall into place.'

'I now know why you're my best friend.'

'I love you, too. But this is going to be tough love. The first thing you have to do is put the chocolate spread in the bin—with all the other comfort food you're addicted to.'

'If it was that easy,' Dodie said, 'you'd be out of business.'

'All right, all right. Don't fret. Cinderella will go to the ball. I'll find you someone who'll keep you at it. Angie. She's your girl. She'll not only monitor your progress but clean the junk food out of your cupboards and be a friend on the end of the phone when you're tempted by a triple cheeseburger with French fries.'

'At the end of the phone won't work. She'll have to be here to forcibly remove them from my fingers.'

'Angie has a husband and kids of her own to babysit. She can't babysit you.'

Dodie caught her breath. What on earth was the matter with her? 'No, no, of course not. I'm sorry. I'm being unreasonable.'

'No, you're in a state. In your shoes I'd be in a state, too. But Angie will do everything else I'd do, and if you just listen to her—'

'You're a star, Gina.'

'She can only do so much. The sweat, pain and tears are down to you. And there'll be plenty of those. If you want to turn heads it's going to take more than cutting out the comfort food. You're going to have to exercise.'

'Cheers.'

'My pleasure. Present yourself at the health club at eight o'clock tomorrow morning. Angie will take a ''before'' picture of you to stick on your fridge door as a deterrent against backsliding. To get the ''after'', you have to do everything she says. No argument.'

'That's all very well, but how am I going to pay for this new life?'

'Oh, I *see*. The only reason you want me to supervise your regime is because I'd do for love, is that it?'

'I'm an artist—'

'But not a starving one, apparently. You're far more likely to keep on the straight and narrow if it's costing you. But,' she went on quickly, cutting off a squeal of pain from Dodie's wallet, 'if you stick to the regime and don't break the zipper on the two-sizes-smaller dress on the big day, I'll give you a special deal.'

'Gina, you're the best—'

'A three-month free membership of the health club, use of all the facilities and the services of a personal trainer.'

'But that's—'

'In return, you can design and make a textile hanging for the health club. Something that reflects the spirit of the place. There's a large empty wall in Reception simply crying out for a Dodie Layton.'

'Ouch.'

'I know. Lake Spa is getting the best of the deal. But this is business, and I have to repay the boss-man's faith in me. Of course, if you don't shape up, I'll forget the textile and charge you the going rate. Believe me, you can't afford it.'

Actually, Dodie realised—given ten seconds to consider the matter—having one of her works on permanent display in a place used by people with high disposable incomes was a win-win situation for her. It gave her a double reason to shape up.

She'd undoubtedly need both of them. She grinned. Gina wasn't just a whip-slender body. She had motivation down to a fine art.

'You've got a deal. I'll bring the digital camera with me tomorrow and take some pictures. I can work on some ideas while you're away.'

'Excellent.' Before Dodie could respond, she added, 'Oh, and make sure that invitation is on my doormat when I return. If Charles Gray isn't bowled over by your smile, I'm planning on being second in line.'

'Problem?'

Brad Morgan had been staring out of the window of his penthouse office for the last twenty minutes.

'What makes you think I've got a problem?' he said, without turning around, as his secretary placed a cup of coffee on his desk.

'Your body's here, but it seems to me that just lately your mind's been somewhere else. Want to talk about it?'

'No, thanks.'

'Is it a woman?' she asked, undeterred.

'Women aren't a problem unless you allow them to be.'

'My mistake. Yours don't stay around long enough to cause trouble. You change yours with the season, the way some women change their wardrobes.'

'At least I'm consistent.'

'Right. They're all tall, thin and looking for a man to show them off in all the right places,' she said dismissively. 'And you're tall, rich and obliging. Temporarily. Is it Lake Spa?' she persisted. 'Is that why you're going down there for the next few weeks?'

'No, Lake Spa is already outperforming expectations, but new buildings inevitably have teething problems and someone needs to be on the spot while Gina's away.'

'You?' She didn't bother to conceal her disbelief.

'Yes, all right, you've seen right through me as usual. I want to take a close look at the staff she's chosen.' He swung his chair around to face her. 'They'll tell me a lot about the woman. And if what they tell me is as good as I think it will be, I want to see who performs above expectations, looks like a natural successor.'

'To Gina? But I thought she was a real find.'

'She is. I'm considering promoting her to take overall charge of the health club division within the year.' He glanced up at her. 'Why don't you take a break and come down for a day or two? See what you think of the hotel now it's finished. Swim, have a sauna, an aromatherapy massage. A complete makeover in the salon. Whatever you like.'

She pulled a face. 'No, thanks. I made myself a promise that I'd never take my clothes off during working hours and it's served me very well for the last thirty years. Why don't you take one of those women who don't give you any trouble? I'm sure they'd queue up for the chance.'

'Like you, Penny, I never mix business with pleasure.' And health and leisure were big business these days. Of course, it helped that he'd applied the same single-minded determination to building his business empire that he'd put into his glorious, if short-lived, career on the rugby field. Expanding fast enough was the only problem there.

'Okay, I give up. Not business. Not women. When was the last time you took a holiday?'

'I hate holidays. There's nothing wrong, okay?' he said, noticing her raised eyebrows. 'It's always the same when a new project reaches completion. A sudden gaping hole in the working day. A what-was-I-doing-before-I-did-that? emptiness.' Lake Spa had been bigger than anything he'd done before. The low was correspondingly deeper, that was all.

'You need a new project. A new challenge.'

'Do I?' How many new challenges were there in his business? The Lake Spa project had been a new direction, combining hotel, health club and conference centre. So what was left?

He'd reached the pinnacle in his sport for one dazzling moment of fame and glory before his career had been cut short by injury. He'd never had a chance to get bored, to reach the been-there, done-that stage when repetition was all he could hope for.

And the journalists watched for signs of him passing his peak.

Not that it had seemed like a plus at the time. He'd had to pull himself back from the edge of despair and start again, this time in business. But now his leisure company had reached a point where all he could do was add another new health club to the chain, another new hotel, another new conference centre. Or another spa.

The prospect of repetition yawned before him. Been there. Done that.

'You definitely need a holiday,' Penny said. 'Something to recharge the batteries. Inspire you.'

What he needed was a challenge that wouldn't leave him empty when it was done. Something that would continue to grow. Keep him focused.

'Inspiration can't be found lying on a beach,' he said. Or staring out of his office window. 'But, if there's nothing needing my attention, I might as well go home.'

Maybe a couple of weeks at the Lake, at the sharp end of his empire, would give him some new ideas.

Dodie resisted the urge to dip her finger in the jar of chocolate spread and instead tossed it into the bin. 'I will be good,' she said out loud to no one in particular, avoiding her reflection as she passed the mirror on her way out to her studio. 'Honest.'

She switched on her computer and, as she waited for it to boot up, tied her hair back in a scrunchie to keep it out of her face. Working at home had a lot of pluses. That she didn't have to wear a suit or tights came top of the list. No need for serious work on her hair first thing in the morning was good, too.

No distractions in the way of sexily helpless men who didn't know how to boil a kettle, or any of the hundred and one other things that a woman will do for a man who says he loves her.

But—and what a nasty word *that* was—there was always a downside to everything.

She might be able to work her own hours, wear what she wanted, not have to bother with make-up except when she was meeting a client, and never, never have to walk to work in the rain.

But there was no doubt that walking away from Martin, along with her post as tutor at Melchester University's Art Department, hadn't helped the constant struggle to keep her weight down.

Her freelance work had increased a little now that she had all the time in the world to concentrate on it, with no students, no man to distract her. But so had her need for comfort food.

Without the brisk daily walk to counter the effect of sitting at her computer and workbench—with exercise an optional extra that she never opted for—the effect on her backside had been disastrous.

Natasha's wedding, she decided, had come just in time to get her back on the rails and maybe even into her favourite black dress. The one that now gaped unattractively over her bust.

The prospect of following her newly wed sister down the aisle on the arm of the thoroughly gorgeous Charles Gray had to be incentive enough for even the most ordinary woman, the most slothful food junkie, to get back into shape.

That and, of course, the opportunity to show Martin just how big a mistake he'd made.

Lake Spa blended perfectly into its surroundings. A series of low-rise stone buildings, each guest room with its own private deck built out over the water, it was set along the edge of an artificial lake which had been created by long-abandoned gravel workings.

Serene, peaceful now, colonised by wild duck and swans, it was light years from the local authority evening classes in aerobics run by Gina before she'd finally married her day job to her passion.

Dodie parked her ancient van—the battered exterior disguised by her own vivid artwork and hideously out of place amongst the top-of-the-range motors that filled the car park—and walked across to a small dock with a little flotilla of sailing dinghies, seeking inspiration for her part of the bargain. She spent far too long taking photographs of the hotel lodge, the conference arena, the health club and lake with her digital camera. Putting off the moment of no return for as long as possible.

Finally, however, she crossed to the entrance, trying not to feel completely overawed by the healthy creatures who, having been for an early-morning swim or session in the gym, were now vibrating with energy as they bounded off to start their day's work.

Overawed by the glossy receptionists, busy with the phones and new arrivals. By the tanned, terrifyingly fit staff, in their health club uniform of dark red tracksuits and perfect smiles.

She came to an abrupt halt in the middle of

Reception. She couldn't do this. It had been a serious mistake to think she could. This was not her kind of place. She began to back towards the door before she was pounced on by Angie, chained to some terrifying machine and exercised without mercy until she was fit and thin, too.

She'd stick to the diet her mother had somehow found time in her busy schedule to deliver personally—doubtless to avoid any lame excuses from her ugly duckling daughter that it hadn't arrived—along with a pair of scales and a gallon of cabbage soup to get her started. And a lecture on how important this was for Natasha. How *kind* she was being when she could have chosen *anyone*—and for 'anyone' Dodie read anyone thin, beautiful and equally famous—to be her bridesmaid. But she'd insisted on having her sister.

So, she'd stick to the diet. Walk to the shops. Fast. Throw away the monster-size bag of mints that lived in her desk drawer, she promised herself guiltily. She could do it. She knew she had the will-power. Somewhere. If she could only remember where she'd left it…

And then, as her feet became entangled with the straps of a sports bag set down momentarily while its owner tightened his shoelaces, she stopped worrying about losing weight, impressing Charles Gray or making Martin wish he'd taken the longer view. She had a more immediate problem.

Staying on her feet.

She flailed wildly with her arms in an attempt to keep her balance, but even as she bowed to the inevitable, accepting that nothing could save her, she crashed into a pair of strong hands. They gripped and held her as she collided with what seemed like a brick wall.

The guy whose designer bag she'd fallen over picked it up, brushed it off and glared at her before walking off without a word.

'Sorry,' she called after him. 'I hope I didn't damage your lovely bag. Bruise it or anything.' Then, as the door closed behind him, 'Poser.'

'Possibly.' The owner of the hands said coolly, and set her back on her feet as if she weighed nothing at all, keeping hold of her while her bones remembered what they were for. 'But perhaps if you'd been looking where you were going—'

Oh, great. Now she was going to get a lecture on pedestrian safety.

'You're right,' she said, in an attempt to forestall it. 'I'm a complete idiot. It's a good job I've no intention of applying for permanent membership here or I'd be rejected as a danger to designer label leather goods.' And, having got that off her chest, she remembered her manners and turned to thank him. She'd undoubtedly have bruises on the fleshy part of her arm where his fingers had gripped her, but that had to be better than the alternative. 'Thank you for catching me,' she said politely.

'Any time,' he said, with just the possibility of a smile.

'I think we'll leave it at just the once, thanks all the same.' Although now she was over the shock, and had had a chance to look more closely at the man who'd stopped her from making a total prat of herself, she was prepared to reconsider.

He was tall, rangy, built for speed rather than heavily muscled, although anyone who could catch her mid-fall and, more importantly, hold on to her, had to be strong. He was certainly a lot more substantial than the young men who, with their slicked-back hair and Armani suits, bounded up the stairs to the restaurant for a healthy breakfast after their early-morning keep-fit sessions.

Maybe that was because he wasn't young. He was well into his thirties, at a guess, and there was a maturity about his body, about his entire bearing, that made them look like callow youths.

His face had a seriously lived-in look that added character by the bucket-load, along with a sprinkling of grey to leaven his thick dark hair.

Not that he wouldn't give the younger men a run for their money in the body department. His suits wouldn't need any skilful padding to make his shoulders look impressive. In a washed-thin T-shirt that left his sinewy arms bare and clung to his shoulders and torso, outlining his form, she could see that they *were* impressive...

'This is your first visit?' he asked, cutting off this unexpected direction to her thoughts. Of course she was an artist. She appreciated...um...*form.* He'd make a wonderful subject for a life class. The blue eyes were a plus, too. 'Don't let one bad experience put you off joining. We're not all posers.' He didn't wait for her to agree with him, but said, 'Do you need some help? Someone to show you around?'

'Oh, no,' she said. Then, realising that she was letting him walk away, 'At least...'

'Yes?' he offered, as if he knew exactly what she was thinking.

'Nothing,' she snapped. Then, 'I'm sorry. I'm nervous. I'm not used to this kind of thing.' She made a gesture that took in a couple of long-legged girls as they crossed the reception area and headed for the exit, dark glossy hair swinging, make-up perfect.

Big mistake.

Her own mousy-coloured hair was tied back in the first scrunchie that had come to hand—one adorned with a cartoon tiger. Cute—she hadn't been able to resist it when she'd seen it in the supermarket—but not particularly grown-up she realised belatedly.

She hadn't thought to apply more than moisturiser to her face either: it was far too early to get actively involved in anything as physical as *thinking*, and wearing make-up to a workout had to be a mistake, surely?

But as his eyes followed the girls, too, and lingered, she had plenty of time to regret her *laissez faire* approach to grooming. He was looking at them the way she'd been hoping Charles Gray might look at her—just long enough for the photographer to get a shot of them both, anyway. With interest.

She clearly needed a lot of work if that was to happen, and if those girls were anything to judge by this was the right place to get it. Pulling herself together, she said, 'I'd better go and tell the receptionist I'm here.'

'I'll leave you to it, then. And relax. This is supposed to be fun.'

'Is it? Really?'

'Really.' He nodded and turned away, and she

saw that despite the honed physique he was favouring his right leg.

'Oh!'

He stopped, looked back. 'Yes?'

'Did I hurt you when I crashed into you?' Her and her big mouth, making sarcastic comments about that idiot and his precious bag instead of making sure she'd done no worse damage. 'I'm so *sorry*—'

The muscles in his jaw tightened briefly. 'It's an old injury,' he said. 'Nothing to do with you.'

'Well, thank goodness for that!' Then, as she realised how that sounded, 'No! I didn't mean...'

But he hadn't waited for her to drivel embarrassingly on.

He'd pushed open the doors that cut off the luxury of the carpeted reception area from the polished wood flooring of the business part of the health club and disappeared.

CHAPTER TWO

'OH, RATS,' Dodie muttered as the doors swung silently back into place. He was sensitive about his limp and her mouth matched her body. They were both too big.

At least she could do something about the body. And, stowing a totally out of proportion feeling of regret that she'd upset him, she took a deep breath and crossed to the reception desk.

'Hi, I'm Dodie Layton. Gina said if I stopped by this morning she'd have organised a new body for me. I put in an order for two sizes smaller?' she offered. 'And a couple of inches taller.' If they were dealing in fantasy she might as well make it a thoroughly worthwhile fantasy. 'She's probably left it in her office for me to pick up.'

'I'm sorry?'

Oh, good grief. She really would have to start taking this seriously. 'No, I'm sorry. Let's start again. Hi, I'm Dodie Layton. Gina has organised an exercise regime for me and a personal trainer to make sure I stick to it,' she offered. 'Angie?'

'*You're* Natasha Layton's sister?'

The girl's apparent disbelief came as no surprise. She'd been seeing disappointment in people's eyes ever since her little sister had graduated from an endless round of dancing, voice and drama classes and

27

stepped into the limelight. Comparisons might be odious, but they were inevitable.

'Yes, I'm Natasha Layton's sister,' she said, trying not to grit her teeth. Shorter, plumper, older. Their hair was the same colour, though. Of course these days Nat had something very expensive done to hers, and it looked as if the sun was shining through it even when it was raining.

That Dodie was the designer of award-winning textiles, an artist, teacher—okay, former teacher—and a person in her own right, never seemed to occur to anyone.

She didn't envy her sister. Would hate her life. Being on show all the time. Knowing that she couldn't nip out to the shops for a bag of doughnuts without a full make-up job unless she wanted to see pictures of herself *déshabillé* in the tabloid press—worse, almost, than being snapped topless through a long lens on a secluded beach. Both of which had happened.

But she wouldn't be human if she didn't long for someone, just once, to say to Natasha, ''You mean you're Dodie Layton's sister? Wow!'

Not in this world.

'If you'd just like to fill in this form,' the receptionist said, looking at her as if wondering how two sisters could be so very different. 'It's for temporary membership. We need it for insurance. While you're doing that I'll go and see if I can find Angie.'

Brad put down the telephone, made a note and sat back in the chair, digging his fingers into the ache in his knee, jarred into life as he'd caught hold of that crazy woman when she crashed into him.

Crazy, but decidedly pretty in a Rubenesque fashion. He frowned. There was something familiar about her, but he'd have remembered if they'd met before.

He found himself grinning. She wasn't the kind of woman you'd forget.

'Oh, Brad. I thought you'd gone through into the gym.'

'On my way. I just stopped to answer the telephone.' He glanced at the receptionist dithering nervously in the doorway and noticed that she was clutching a file. 'Do you need help with something, Lucy?'

'Oh, no. I was just looking for Angie. Have you seen her? Gina asked her to act as personal trainer to a special client—'

'That was Angie's husband on the phone. She's been rushed into hospital with suspected appendicitis. Organise some flowers, will you?'

'No problem. What about her schedule, though? Her classes?' Then, 'What about Miss Layton?'

'Why don't you see what you can sort out with her classes?' he said, pushing the girl back on her own resources. 'I'll talk to Miss Layton.' He held out his hand for the file.

Dodie glanced up as the receptionist returned. 'Hold onto that,' she said, as she offered her the form. 'You can give it to Brad. If you'll come through to the office?'

'Brad? Who's Brad? What happened to Angie?'

'She's off sick.'

'At a health club? Is that allowed?'

'It's this way,' she said, without comment. Dodie followed, smacking her own wrist. There was nothing funny about keeping fit, she chided herself. She'd have to stow her sense of humour for the duration. 'Brad, this is Gina's friend. Dodie Layton.'

The receptionist stepped back, holding the door wide so that she could get through, then closed it behind her. Leaving her alone with the guy with the seriously buff body and the good catching hands. She could still feel the imprint of them where he'd grabbed her.

It was clearly going to be one of those days.

'Hello again,' she said.

He'd been looking at some notes in an open file on the desk. He didn't actually flinch as he glanced up with the beginnings of a smile curving a mouth that was as promising as his body. But he did look at her for what seemed like the longest five seconds in the history of the world before indicating the chair facing his desk.

'Come in, Miss Layton.'

'Dodie,' she said, staying where she was. People only called her 'Miss Layton' when they were going to say something unpleasant.

'Dodie. You're a friend of Gina's?' he said, picking up on the receptionist's comment.

'We dabbled in the same fingerpaint at nursery school,' she said. 'I stayed with the paint while Gina discovered the jungle gym. The rest, as they say, is history. And you are?'

'Brad Morgan. Do you want to take a seat while I check out the notes Gina left for Angie?'

'Won't I burn more calories standing up? I haven't got much time to get into shape.'

'I don't believe it will make a significant difference,' he said. 'Would you like some coffee?'

'Coffee?' Things were looking up, she thought as she crossed to the chair and sat down. 'Is that allowed?'

'It's not encouraged,' he admitted. 'But—'

'You don't believe it will make a significant difference.' That smile almost broke out of its restraints. He made a valiant effort to keep it under control, however. 'I'll pass, thanks.' She'd taken the precaution of tanking up on caffeine before leaving home. And she smiled at him—the wide-screen version—just to show him how it should be done. 'I didn't realise you work here.'

He looked as if he was about to say something, but changed his mind. 'Don't let the limp fool you. I could make you sweat if I put my mind to it.'

Mr Sensitive wouldn't have to put her through a full body workout to make her sweat. He was raising her temperature just by looking at her. She was beginning to take a serious dislike to the man; she wasn't the one who'd made an issue of his dodgy leg. In fact, she was beginning to wish he'd looked the other way when she'd stumbled and just let her fall.

She didn't say that.

Instead, with a gesture that took in his worn grey sweats, she said, 'I simply meant that you don't quite fit the glossy corporate image.' Then, because she always said too much when she was nervous, 'Is your good tracksuit in the wash?'

Brad bit back a sudden urge to grin. Dodie Layton was overweight, out of condition and, with her just-keeping-it-out-of-my-eyes hairstyle, lack of make-up and unpolished nails, she seemed to have completely bypassed the notion of 'perfect grooming'.

Her attitude, however, was refreshing. Stimulating, even. He felt stimulated to eject her from his state-of-the-art health club. She didn't fit the image. She was making the place look untidy.

On the other hand it had been a long time since anyone had spoken to him without any thought for the consequences. Or weighing up the impression they were making. Apparently she didn't care what kind of impression she was making—at least, not on him.

And wasn't the whole point of his health club chain to help people like her *achieve* the 'image'?

He held out his hand for her temporary membership form. 'I'll take that, shall I?'

He wasn't entirely sure what was going on, or why Gina was apparently giving this woman the run of the place without expecting her to pay for membership, but he decided to go along with it for the time being.

'I see from Gina's notes that you're hoping to lose

a couple of dress sizes.' An interesting way of putting it.

'Not *hoping*. It's absolutely vital that I can get into a size...' She stopped, apparently unwilling to betray her present dress size. 'Something smaller.'

'And you've got six weeks?' When she didn't answer, he looked up. She did not look happy. 'Have I got that wrong?'

'No. Yes...'

He sat back. 'Perhaps you'd like some time to consider the question?' he offered.

'No. The thing is I did tell Gina six weeks. But my mother called round this morning and apparently the final fitting for the dress is much sooner than that.'

'Fitting?' He frowned. Dress? 'You're getting married?'

She flushed. 'Does it sound that unlikely?'

'Not at all,' he said, instantly regretting his tone. It wasn't for him to suggest she wouldn't make some man a wonderful wife. He was sure that on a good day she was a person of infinite warmth and charm. Today just wasn't a good day.

But weddings were not his favourite subject and it was beginning to feel as if this woman had been sent especially to torment him.

The sparkle in her large, dark eyes would drag a response from even the most unwilling of men, however. Looking at her, flustered and furious with him, he felt a compelling urge to put his arms around her and give her a cuddle. Found himself wishing he'd taken the opportunity when she was shaky and vulnerable.

Unlikely that she was getting married? No, he decided. Despite everything, he conceded that it was not unlikely at all.

'But you're not wearing a ring,' he pointed out, rather more gently, by way of apology. 'And you have left it rather late to get into shape for your big day.' Unless of course it was a rush job. His stomach clenched unexpectedly at the thought as he glanced at the form again. The section on medical conditions had been left blank, but there was no point in pussy-footing about. 'If you're pregnant, you should have mentioned it on the form.'

'Well, thanks,' she snapped. Abruptly the sparkle disappeared, leaving him with the impression that the sun had gone behind a cloud. She was clearly not amused by his less than tactful comment on her shape. 'But for your information it's my sister who's fallen for the happy ever after bit. Being older, I've got a better idea of the reality. I've simply been drafted in to make sure the pageboys don't put white mice down the necks of the flower girls. At least not in church. I'm chief bridesmaid,' she added, presumably in case he was not only rude, but slow on the uptake.

Firmly put in his place, and oddly pleased to be there, he said, 'That sounds like fun.'

'It sounds like hard work to me. And if I have to be hampered by a floor-length dress made from a fabric totally unsuitable for child-minding, it would help if it didn't split under the strain. Should I have to make any sudden moves.' Then, like a ray of sunshine peeping out from behind a storm cloud, her apparently irrepressible smile was heralded by the appearance of a dimple. 'Virtue, however, is its own reward. It won't all be sticky fingers and nervous vomiting. Traditionally the chief bridesmaid gets the best man...' The flush returned, hotter and pinker, as she ground to a halt.

She was *blushing*? How delightful. How unexpected. She had to be—what? He glanced at the form. She'd given her age as twenty-six. If she'd been in the same school year as Gina he could add at least a year to that. Maybe two. Which suggested any other figures she'd put down were suspect, too.

'I've got the picture,' he said. 'You believe the best man will be more receptive to your ample charms if they are a little less...'

It occurred to him, somewhat belatedly, that he wasn't having a particularly good day either, and he stopped before he said something he might have cause to regret.

'Ample?' she offered, not letting him off the hook. She didn't wait for an answer, but leaned forward to retrieve her diary from the roomy canvas bag she'd dropped at her feet. As he was confronted with a glimpse of her generous cleavage, a hint of smooth, soft breasts a man could lose himself in, he found that his mouth dried. Seemingly unaware of the effect she had caused, she flipped through the diary until she found the entry she was looking for. 'D-Day is the thirtieth April.' She looked up. 'That's D for Dress,' she said. 'Can it be done?'

Her mouth was innocent of lipstick, but it was full
and inviting—like the rest of her—and defied all at-
tempts by its owner to keep it under control. Again,
like the rest of her.

'Three weeks…' he said, making a determined effort to get his mind on the matter in hand. 'Seven-
pound weight loss on a sensible diet. Maybe a little
more if you have seriously bad eating habits.'

'I'm banking on twenty.'

'We don't encourage crash dieting—it isn't safe
and you won't keep the weight off. But exercise will
help tone everything up, which should do the rest.
If you work hard enough.' He forced himself to re-
gard her sternly. 'How badly do you want this?'

'How badly?'

'I can see the appeal of slimming down for the
big occasion—' although the attraction of dressing
up in impractical and outdated clothes simply to witness two people make fools of themselves seemed
to have passed him by '—but I'd be happier if you
were taking a long-term approach to fitness.'

'Look, I've discussed this with Gina. Your boss?'
she reminded him.

'My boss?'

'I've had the pep talk, okay?'

He swallowed a smile.

'Okay,' he said. 'I just didn't want you making
yourself thoroughly miserable in an effort to fit a
smaller dress size. Just for one day.'

'*Just?*' She leaned forward so that her cleavage
was once again an unconscious invitation that any
man would be delighted to accept. 'Let me tell you

this isn't just any old day. I may not be the bride, but if I explain that the best man is going to be Charles Gray, would that clarify the importance of a smaller dress size?'

'Charles Gray?' he queried, distracted.

'You're kidding, right?'

He dragged his gaze back to her face. 'Sorry.'

'Actor?' she offered. 'Movie star? Dark brown eyes that crinkle dangerously at the corner whenever he smiles, floppy corn-coloured hair and a seriously cute bottom—' She frowned. 'Unless of course he used a body double in that movie where he and—'

'Okay,' he said abruptly, stopping her before she started drooling. 'I'm with you.' He'd heard of Charles Gray. It just hadn't occurred to him to connect Dodie Layton with a pin-up movie star with whom the entire female population appeared to have fallen in love. 'I can quite see that as a reward for keeping the pageboys in order he'd be exactly what the bridesmaid ordered.'

'Absolutely.' Her dark eyes flashed dangerously. 'Although I prefer to think that I'm *his* reward for not losing the ring.'

It was the flash that flipped the 'on' switch in his brain and the name finally connected.

Dodie *Layton*.

'Your sister is Natasha Layton?' There had been a photograph of her on the front page of his morning newspaper. Even the broadsheets were treating the announcement of her forthcoming marriage as a major news story. 'I'm sorry, I didn't make the connection.'

'Don't apologise. It comes as a shock to most people. Even my mother finds it difficult to believe we're out of the same gene pool.'

'On the contrary. I thought you seemed familiar when we met out there. There's a family likeness.'

She gave him a look that suggested she wasn't convinced, but now he knew they were sisters he could see that they shared the same dark, expressive eyes. It was possible they shared the same fine bone structure, but in Dodie's case the effect was slightly blurred.

Something she wanted to fix, it seemed. In a hurry.

For Charles Gray.

At least the reason Gina had given her the freedom of Lake Spa was now clear. He'd had a momentary concern that he'd misjudged the woman. That she was using her position to give her friends the run of the place.

But she'd marked the file 'Special Deal' and left a note for Angie to take 'before', 'during' and 'after' photographs. He knew that a lot of people liked to have those, but Dodie Layton was obviously getting the use of Lake Spa in return for a sweet little "transformation" piece in one of the women's magazines.

He could see that though Dodie and Gina might be friends, this was business. Good business. For both of them.

Gina was getting an opportunity to impress him with the kind of publicity that couldn't be bought. The gossip magazine that was paying for exclusive coverage of the wedding—and there undoubtedly would be one—would leap at the chance to cover the human interest side-story of the Cinderella sister.

Their rivals would probably pay even more handsomely to get a piece of the action, too and it didn't take much imagination to guess the photographs.

Dodie in outsize jogging pants, her hair tied up in a childish scrunchie that was decorated with some soft furry animal. She'd obviously chosen the least flattering clothes she could lay her hands to in order to emphasise the transformation.

Unflattering pictures of her working up a sweat, suffering in the name of beauty—all with the Lake Spa logo in plain sight—would be worth the reward of a photograph of her transformed into a wedding belle and dancing with the man of every woman's dreams.

There was only one problem. With Angie in hospital they were short of a fairy godmother to perform the transformation. On the point of calling through to Reception for the diary, to see who could fit her in, he hesitated.

This would need careful handling. The Natasha Layton wedding would be a media feeding frenzy. Gina had chosen her own staff and, in her absence, had undoubtedly picked someone she could trust to be completely discreet. He didn't know any of them well enough to judge who on the team would be capable of keeping this kind of secret, even from a partner. He doubted that any of them could.

Besides, if Dodie had any hope of achieving her objective in such a short time she'd need a dedicated staff member to see her through. Total support.

He was the only person around here with a clear

diary: the only person he could be sure wouldn't share this interesting piece of pillow talk. And, since everything seemed to be running like clockwork—apart from Angie's dash to Emergency—he could do with something to keep him occupied.

'Right,' he said. 'We'd better get started. There's a lot to do if Mr Gray's reward is going to be worthy of his, um, "cute" bottom.' Which took the sparkle out of her smile, he thought as he stood up. Got those expressive eyes flashing like a lighthouse. Which was good. Anger got the adrenalin flowing. His own, for some reason, seemed to be in flood. 'Let's get you measured up and weighed, and take some photographs.'

She pulled a face.

'It won't hurt a bit,' he promised.

'How would you know?'

He thought about the photographs that had graced the newspapers years ago, when he'd left the rugby field on a stretcher. How much he'd hated seeing himself like that. Helpless. His leg in ruins.

'I know,' he said. He'd used that photograph, blown up massively, to drive himself to greater efforts with physiotherapy after each operation. 'You can stick it on your fridge door afterwards. It'll help keep you on the straight and narrow long after your encounter with Charles Gray is nothing but a cherished memory to tell your grandchildren.'

'Thanks, but I'd rather put a photograph of Charles Gray in such a prominent place. He's prettier.'

'Whatever works for you,' he said, refusing to

flatter her. She'd have to work for every word of praise. 'This way,' he said, heading for the door.

'No, wait—' He opened the door and pointedly held it for her. 'You mean you're…' She'd swivelled around in the chair but was making no attempt to follow him. '*You're* going to be my personal trainer?'

'Is that a problem? I'm afraid without Angie it's a question of all hands to the pumps—'

'Liposuction!' she exclaimed, clasping her hands in front of her. 'That's it! You're a genius!'

Since she was obviously just playing for time, he made no comment.

'No good, huh?'

'I'm afraid not. Vacuuming up the fat only works if it's in one place. You're just going to have to tone up the flesh you've got. All over.'

'*Just?* What is this with you and "just"? Have you any idea how much flesh there is?' she demanded.

'I'm about to find out. After that, if you do everything I tell you—cut out—' it didn't take instant recall to repeat Gina's list of her friend's weaknesses '—chocolate, cheeseburgers, doughnuts—'

'Give me that!' she exclaimed, as she made a dive for the folder. 'Whatever Gina wrote in there is a lie!'

Brad lifted the folder out of her reach and caught her as she crashed into him. He was expecting it so there was no damage. In fact, as he caught her round her waist to steady them both, and was assailed by the wholesome scents of shampoo and fabric conditioner, he took full advantage of his second opportunity to hold her. It felt good. There was something appealing, something feminine about her that was missing in the starved thin models who usually occupied that space.

'—and start taking a little gentle exercise,' he continued, 'Mr Gray won't know what's…um…*hit* him. Or maybe you'll manage not to fall over him, or flatten him.'

Okay, he was lying about the 'gentle'. He wasn't the kind of fairy godfather who made wishes come true with a magic wand. The only way he knew was to reach out and grab what you wanted for yourself. The hard way. The way he'd done it himself.

The way he was holding onto Dodie Layton right now, her voluptuous curves pressed hard against his chest.

He disentangled himself with reluctance, but her mind was fixed on the very pretty Charles Gray. Not on a wrecked rugby player.

'You just have to ask yourself if you really, really want to headline in the gossip magazines. Be the woman in the photograph captioned, *Charles Gray Loses his Heart to the Bride's Lovely Sister*,' he said.

It was a little like worrying a bad tooth. Stupid, but impossible to resist.

'You disapprove?'

Confronted, he could not deny it. He did disapprove. Not of her desire to get into shape—although he was beginning to see real possibilities in the shape she had. Just the reason for it. But she was a grown woman. If she wanted to make a fool of herself it wasn't his business to stop her. It was his business to take advantage of the situation.

'Why would I disapprove?' he enquired coolly. 'You want to get fit.'

'But you disapprove of the motivation. Kiss-chase is perfectly okay when it's a man doing the chasing, but it's not quite *nice* for a woman to set her sights on an especially tempting target and be totally honest about it.'

'Look—'

'No, you look, Mr Morgan—'

'Brad,' he insisted, really, really hating the way she'd called him 'Mr Morgan' to press home her point.

'Okay, Brad,' she said encouragingly. 'I need you to use your imagination here. I want you to consider a slightly different scenario. Same big showbiz wedding, right? Only this time *you're* going to be the best man.'

'I don't quite see—'

'Are you with me?' she insisted.

He shrugged, refusing to commit himself.

'Right,' she said, taking that as a yes. 'Now, then, Mr Best Man, you've just learned that my sister— the utterly lovely and very desirable Natasha Layton—is going to be the bridesmaid.' She cocked a glossy dark brow at him. 'Think about it.'

He thought about it.

According to the media, Natasha Layton had been at the top of every red-blooded male's fantasy wish list since she'd made her first film. She was not only beautiful, in an ice-cool, untouchably perfect way— a way that made men long to muss her up—but a supremely talented actress. Dodie was suggesting that, given that scenario, he'd be the one planning sweet seduction and no one would think any the worse of him for it. Would expect it, in fact. Would envy him the chance to be that close to a legend, even if he did nothing more than kiss her hand.

He didn't have much truck with fantasies, but he did have an imagination—one that could see how tough it would be if you were Natasha Layton's older, earthier sister. Having to cope with the undisguised astonishment that you were related. Over and over again.

If Dodie Layton wanted her own fifteen minutes of fame then who was he to begrudge it to her? Especially when it was going to provide Lake Spa and the rest of his health club chain with a public relations coup.

Whether, in the long run, she'd be happy, was a moot point. It seemed to him that this might very well come under the heading of 'be careful what you wish for'. But it was her wish. Her dream to be swept away by Prince Charming.

'You're making the point that this is the age of equal opportunities in all things? Including fantasy?'

'You see?' she said, with a big smile. 'That wasn't so difficult, was it?'

More difficult than it should have been. But what she did with her life was her own business. It was a long time since women had sat back and waited for a hunter to single them out of the herd. If they ever had.

'Sorry. I guess I'm just a sweet old-fashioned kind of man.'

'Oh, right. You've never been chased—and caught—by a woman with one thing on her mind?'

Before he could think of an answer that didn't make a liar out of him, she held up her hand. 'Sorry. Sweet, old-fashioned men never kiss and tell.'

'That's right, Miss Layton. We never do.' Then, he added, 'Tell.'

But as he connected with Dodie's sudden grin his heart, for the first time in as long as he could remember, lifted a beat and he found himself sorely tempted to cradle her head in his hand and very slowly lower his mouth to her smiling lips. Show her just how sweet, old-fashioned men kissed. And never told.

Just to prove the point.

He restrained himself, but with rather more difficulty than was quite comfortable. It wasn't just his heart that had lifted.

'In the meantime you've got a lot of hard work to get through before you find out if Charles Gray knows how to keep a lady's secrets,' he said, more sharply than he'd intended. But maybe that wasn't such a bad thing, because her grin faded faster than a man's dreams.

Taking advantage of the instant drop in warmth, he took a step back, turned and headed in the direction of the personal trainers' room, leaving her to follow or not.

Her choice.

CHAPTER THREE

DODIE stared after him while she caught her breath. For a moment there she'd been sure he was going to kiss her. For a moment there she had rather hoped he would. Which just proved how risky it was to leave the house with nothing inside her but a bowl of cabbage soup.

At least one *pain au chocolat* was absolutely essential for a clear head, she decided as she gathered her bag and went after him.

She paused at the door to a small office. He'd spread her folder flat on the desk and was standing with his back to her, studying the form she'd filled in and Gina's notes detailing all her little weaknesses. It gave her an opportunity to notice the way his thick hair curled into a little question mark at the nape of his neck. To admire the width of his shoulders, the way his back narrowed into his waist and culminated in the neatest—

'Ready?' he asked, glancing back at her.

'No,' she said. 'But bear with me. I'll catch up as we go along. What do we do first?'

'You jump on the scales. I make a note of your weight.'

She regarded the businesslike balance scales without enthusiasm. She wasn't jumping, stepping or getting on them in any other way he devised. Not until she'd lost a few pounds.

'There's no need for that,' she said firmly, and crossed her fingers behind her back. 'If you look, you'll see that I put my weight on that form I just spent ten minutes completing.'

And then she smiled, just to let him see what a good, truthful person she was.

'Sure you did. You put your age, too.'

And, from beneath heavy lids that veiled eyes the colour of faded denim, Brad Morgan smiled right back at her. His eyes had those yummy crinkly bits at the corners, too. On women they'd be considered ageing, something to be zapped with the latest anti-wrinkle cream. On men they added character and were just, well, yummy. Just one more example of inequality.

Then he straightened. 'Now, shall we see what you really weigh?'

Oh, right. His eyes might crinkle engagingly at the corners, but that was all down to bone structure and the elasticity of his skin. It didn't mean *he* was yummy—in fact she was becoming quite a connoisseur of his smiles.

There was the polite, heaven-help-me smile of a stranger who'd just caught her in mid-air and very much wished he hadn't.

The thoughtful, heaven-help-*her* smile of a man who thought she probably needed counselling.

And the momentary smile that had died to something much more intense in the heartbeat before he'd turned and walked away.

That one had definite possibilities.

This one, she interpreted as a straightforward I-don't-believe-a-word-you're-saying smile.

'That's not nice, Mr Morgan,' she said. 'It suggests you don't trust me.'

'Brad,' he reminded her. 'And it suggests I think you have a problem with numbers. Or your bathroom scales. When did you last have them calibrated?'

'Calibrated?' You were supposed to have them calibrated? 'They're new,' she said. Well, they were. New to her. The fact that they'd been in her mother's bathroom for as long as she could remember was none of his business.

'Not that new,' he suggested. 'The weight you put here is in imperial measurements. Shall we see how you do in metric?'

He wasn't going to take no for an answer, she realised. She could step onto the scales or she could walk. It wasn't negotiable. Shrugging, as if he was the one with a problem, she kicked off her trainers and stepped gingerly onto the platform. He slid the weight along the balance bar. It registered an embarrassing two and a bit kilos heavier than the weight she'd put down. The five pounds she'd deducted from the result of standing on her mother's scales. They were accurate enough, it seemed, despite their age. And lack of calibration.

'Heavens,' she said. 'Just look at that. My scales are obviously way off. I'm going to take them right back to the store.'

'You do that.'

'Unless—'

'Unless?'

'Well, of course,' she said, somewhat recklessly, 'I was naked when I weighed.'

'Were you?' He paused with his pen an inch from the paper and turned his head to look at her.

'Would that have made a difference?'

'Why don't you strip off and we'll see?' he offered. She was almost certain he was smiling, but this was a new one. Something hidden. Unreadable. 'There are no secrets between a woman and her personal trainer.'

If he believed that, she thought, he was an idiot. She didn't think he was an idiot. He was altogether too astute for her liking.

She was the idiot for having mentioned it.

'I don't think so,' she said politely. 'Thank you. I was simply making the point.'

'I'll bear it in mind. Go and stand by the height chart, will you?'

Oh, good grief! She'd exaggerated her height, too. Just the tiniest little bit, to make the height/weight ratio look better. She was a hopeless case. But it was one thing saying that you didn't care whether you were a few pounds overweight, she'd discovered. It was another thing altogether exposing the awful truth. She was clearly a lot vainer than she thought.

'Don't tell me,' he said, as he checked the form against reality. 'Let me guess. You were wearing high heels?'

Her response, 'Doesn't everybody?' earned her a

promising twitch at the corner of his mouth as he opened a drawer. If she could just make him laugh—

'Okay. Arms up.'

'No need for that. I've already surrendered…' Her voice died as he unfurled a tape measure. 'What are you going to do with that?'

He lifted his brows imperceptibly, inviting her to use her imagination.

'You're going to measure me, aren't you?' And she made a wordless gesture to indicate her hips. 'Around here?'

'Around everywhere,' he promised her. 'Before I can organise a training plan I need to see where the excess weight is situated.'

'I should have thought you could *see* that.'

'Hips, thighs, waist,' he agreed, without hesitation.

'There's no need to be kind. I need to reduce everywhere.'

'Not quite everywhere,' he said, quite unable to resist a grin. 'It would be a shame to shrink your natural assets. A low-cut dress and a stop-your-heart bra and I shouldn't think anyone would notice anything else. Not even Mr Gray.'

She groaned. She'd been the first girl to get breasts in her class at school. She'd thought that was embarrassing, but it was nothing compared to the thought of Brad Morgan running a tape around her vital statistics. The only thing worse would be the look of disbelief in the best man's eyes as he compared the bride's sister with the lovely bride.

She kept telling herself she had much the same

measurements as Marilyn Monroe, but it didn't help. Women were being worn thinner these days.

'We'll do this again in seven days and check your progress,' he said, as if that would somehow make her feel better.

'Really, that won't be necessary. I can check my own progress. I'll know things are going well when I can do up my jeans.'

'That's good,' he agreed, but her relief was short-lived. 'However, I prefer a slightly more scientific method. Just in case your jeans are as flexible as your bathroom scales.'

'I won't cheat. I promise. You can trust me.'

'First you have to trust *me*, Dodie. This is a joint effort. We can stop any time. You just have to say.' He gave her an opportunity to do just that, but she didn't say a word. 'We're doing this for you. So that you can feel good about yourself. Enjoy your sister's wedding.' There was another pause that this time seemed to go on for ever. 'Achieve your heart's desire.'

Brad was asking her if she really, really wanted to be the surprise belle of the wedding. A mini-belle, anyway. She had no wish to upstage her sister on her special day. Just to have a reasonably special day of her own.

To know that when the best man kissed her, in time-honoured fashion, he would be congratulating himself on his good luck.

And that when Martin saw the photographs in *Celebrity* he would be kicking himself all around the college. That, more importantly, everyone else would stop feeling sorry for her.

'That is what you really, really want, isn't it?'

She shrugged. Put that way it seemed just a little bit shallow. She wanted more than that. She wanted to regain her self-respect. But confessing that involved baring her soul, and she was already baring more than any woman ever wanted to.

'I'm not very comfortable with exposing my worst secrets in this way,' she said, sidestepping the question. 'I'll try and stop complaining.'

'That would help. If you'd just lift your arms so that we can get this over and done with?'

She took a deep breath. How bad could it be? Without another word she raised her arms, closing her eyes as he stepped up close, reached around to slip the tape around her back, encircling her with his arms.

It was a long time since she'd been so close to a man. Touched by a man. More than a year since she'd walked out on the 'day job' and everything that went with it. Security and common-room companionship, where shared concerns had seemed to offer the perfect basis for a relationship and the opportunities for making a fool of yourself—and being made a fool of—were manifest.

Yet even with her eyes closed she would have known it wasn't a woman running the tape around her bust, her waist... Not that he lingered. He was briskly efficient about his task and she had no complaints. But their closeness brought the intimacy of his breath against her cheek, raising the soft down.

The minty freshness of his toothpaste mingled with subtler masculine scents that clung to his skin and washed over her, stirring something feminine and vulnerable that she'd locked down, hidden away.

'Okay, you can breathe out now,' he said abruptly, as he straightened and tightened the tape around her upper arm.

Breathless, she said, 'Sorry. I'm being such a baby about this.'

'I understand. But I'm afraid this is the "personal" in personal trainer. You probably don't even admit how much you weigh to your best friend.'

Her turn to smile. A rueful one this time. 'I think we both know that I don't even admit that to myself.'

He released the tape. 'I promise you all your secrets are safe with me.'

'Yeah, right. You said.'

He made a final note in the folder. 'I'll just take a couple of photographs now.' He went through the desk drawers, opened a cupboard. 'Or I would if I could find a camera.'

'No problem. I've got mine.' She wanted all this stuff over and done with in one go. She reached down into her bag and handed him her digital camera. 'I'll print out a copy for your file when I've downloaded it onto my computer.' With the images under her control, she realised, she could make herself look as thin as she liked.

He took the camera, looked at it appreciatively. 'Expensive piece of kit.'

'Tax-deductible. I use it for work.' She leaned

closer, switched it on. 'You just point this at me and click here,' she said, pointing to the button. 'It's so simple that a two-year-old could use it.' When he didn't answer she looked up, straight into his eyes. They seemed to be boring into her and she felt herself heating up. 'But if you need any help just say.'

'We'll take them outside,' he said, switching it off and putting it into his pocket. 'Let's stow your bag in a locker, do some gentle stretches and then we can take a walk.'

'A walk?' Not a jog or a run. That didn't sound too bad. 'I can walk,' she said.

'Yes? Well, just make sure you keep going forwards.'

She pulled a face at his back as he went to organise a locker for her. Childish, maybe. But infinitely satisfying.

He was still favouring his injured leg when, after the stretches, she followed him to the exit. 'I can walk, but will you be all right?'

'If I can't keep up, I'll let you know,' he said dryly.

She walked alongside him, watching him for a moment. 'What happened?' she asked. 'To your knee.'

'I went down awkwardly,' he said. 'And then half a dozen men came down on top of me.' Seeing her look of confusion, he said, 'It wasn't deliberate, just one of things that happen in the heat of a game.'

'Game?'

'I played rugby.' She must have looked as sick as

she felt because, with a half-smile, he said, 'It's okay. We won the match.'

'Terrific. That must have made it all worthwhile.'

'At the time it seemed enough.'

'Before you realised how much damage had been done?' He shrugged. 'You see?' she said, coming to a halt. 'Gina is always on at me to get into sports. To play basketball or tennis or something. I keep telling her how dangerous it is.'

'Bad for your elbows, tennis,' he agreed, and finally grinned. 'Come on. This won't hurt much, I promise.' Then, as they made their way down the steps. 'You put "textile designer" as your occupation on your membership form. What does that involve?'

She glanced at him, wondering if he was being sarcastic.

Seeing her expression, he said, 'I'm just trying to get some idea of your working day. I don't get the impression that you spend your day running around a loom.'

Definitely sarcastic.

'I'm a designer—an artist—not a weaver,' she said. 'I don't use a loom. I use my imagination. And a computer.'

'Oh, great. Use a computer. Broaden your backside. And when you're not sitting at your computer?'

'I spend a lot of time looking for suitable materials.'

His eyes narrowed. 'You mean shopping, don't you?'

'There's no fooling you, is there?' she asked.

Then, because her question had been rhetorical, 'It's hard work, shopping. Hunting for just the right texture of cloth, shape and shade of beads, sequins, ribbon. Burns up the calories a treat.'

'Not if your recovery technique involves Danish pastries and cappuccino in the coffee shop afterwards.'

'And then,' she said, ignoring his interjection and ploughing on determinedly, 'when I've got everything I need, I start work. Creating the design I've made.'

'And that involves what, exactly? Sewing?'

Sewing!

She stopped trying to impress him. 'On a really hard day,' she said, 'I have to thread my own sewing machine needle.'

Pushed, she could do sarcastic.

'I'm not trying to be offensive—'

'It just comes naturally, huh?'

'I'm simply attempting to get a picture of your lifestyle.'

'Sedentary?' she offered.

'In that case I want you walking everywhere from now on.'

'Everywhere?' A tiny internal demon urged her to say, 'Even to work?'

'Is it far? You could split it—drive halfway and walk the rest. About a mile should do it.'

'Each way?' she demanded, as if the idea appalled her. And she made a valiant effort not to smile too much as they turned onto the footpath that went around the lake.

'Each way, every day. As you pointed out, you don't have much time. Can you handle that?'

Tough call. She'd have to walk out of her back door, across the courtyard and into her studio. All of ten yards.

'That's a bit harsh, Brad.' She used his name here so that he'd know she was being deeply sincere. 'I'm not sure I can manage that.'

'If you're serious about getting fit, Dodie—' he used exactly the same note of sincerity when he said her name '—I think you're going to have to try. Now, let's walk.'

Brad set off slowly enough, picking up the pace so gradually that she scarcely noticed it until she began to puff. He didn't appear to be walking fast, but his natural stride was a lot longer than hers— not that her stride could be described as natural— and she had to concentrate hard to stop herself putting in the occasional skip just to keep up.

'What about the photographs?' she gasped, after a few minutes of this, hoping that if she reminded him he'd stop so that she could catch her breath. 'This would be a good spot.'

She stopped anyway.

'I'll take them from the other side of the lake,' he said, without slowing.

'The other side?' She looked across the lake. Then at the path that apparently went all around it.

'With Lake Spa in the background,' he called back.

'Very picturesque,' she muttered.

He glanced down at her as she put on a little trot

to catch up. He'd better not try out his repertoire of
smiles on her, that was all, she thought rebelliously.
Why was she *doing* this? Just to impress some man
who probably wouldn't give her a second glance?
Just to impress some other man who had already
demonstrated that he didn't give a damn?

Was she crazy?

Probably.

But she gritted her teeth and kept pace with Brad
for another ten minutes or so until a stitch in her
side became too painful to carry on. She pulled up,
slumped over, her hand at her side.

'That's it,' she gasped. 'You've made your point.
I'm a wreck. Unless you want to carry me back,
you're going to have to stop now.'

'Why on earth didn't you say something before?'
he demanded, taking her elbow, encouraging her to
stand up straight.

'Aren't you supposed to notice?'

'You weren't showing any signs of distress.'
Looking at her, he shook his head. 'Acting clearly
runs in the family. Come on, keep moving. Walk on
the spot to keep the muscles warm.' And, taking her
wrist, he checked her pulse against the second hand
of his wristwatch.

She could feel her blood pounding against his cool
fingers, and as the pain in her side faded she stared
at them. He had big, strong hands, and she found
herself imagining them around a rugby ball, arms at
full stretch as he crashed over the line to score a try.

'Not great, but we'll improve it.'

'What?' She looked up.

He released her wrist. 'Your recovery rate.'

'Oh.'

His own recovery rate gave absolutely no cause for concern, Dodie decided. She could see the steady rise and fall of his chest through the thin T-shirt, a steady counterpoint to the rapid beat of her own heart. He was utterly unruffled by the brisk walk, while she was positively…glowing.

'Okay,' he said, when her breathing was at an acceptable rate. 'You can set the pace from here, but remember, a quiet stroll in the country won't get you in shape. You're going to have to push yourself a little.'

'How little?'

'Well, you should be able to talk while you're walking. Just.'

Talking wasn't a problem. She could handle that. 'So, Brad. How long have you worked here?' she asked, setting off at a gentle pace that she hoped would eventually get her back to base. The distance around the lake seemed a lot further when it wasn't just a pretty scene viewed in repose.

'Here? This is my first day at Lake Spa. That's why you've got me all to yourself.'

'What luck,' she said, and he glanced at her, eyes narrowed. 'What did you do before you came here?' she asked quickly.

'You're not going fast enough,' he warned.

'I thought I was doing pretty well. Any faster and I won't be able to talk.'

'Any slower and you won't get round before dark. And when I said *talk* I didn't mean that you should start a conversation. I want you to be running this by next week.'

'Dream on,' she said.

'It's your dream. I'm just helping you make it come true.' And he raised the pace slightly, leaving her with the curious impression that he didn't want to answer her questions.

Dodie stood beneath the hot needles of water from the power shower and groaned. It was a year since she'd walked anywhere further than the corner Eight 'til Late, where she shopped for fresh bread and milk and chocolate.

She could have bought it all cut price when she did her weekly shop at the supermarket, but at least this way she was forced to leave the cottage every other day. When she was actually working on a commission nothing but the desire for chocolate would shoehorn her out of her workshop. But her quick dash to the corner three times a week had done nothing to prepare her for this.

She'd staggered into the health club barely able to put one foot in front of the other. Brad, having assured her that 'it would get easier', hadn't noticeably raised a sweat, and his limp had been barely discernible as he'd left her to take a shower with instructions to meet him in the restaurant when she was done. He wanted to run through her programme over lunch.

She groaned again at the thought of walking upstairs. Not even the prospect of food helped. She just knew it would be hideously healthy stuff. All bran and lentils.

Maybe there was a lift… No. Stupid thought.

She dug a pair of comfortable cargo pants and a sweatshirt out of the depths of her bag, but by the time she'd dried her hair the effort of tying it back was just too much and she left it loose. This had the advantage of covering at least a small portion of her distressingly pink and shiny face.

Nowhere near enough of it. Brad took one look at her and poured her a glass of water.

'Hungry?' he asked.

'Please don't torment me.' She drank the water and he refilled the glass for her. 'It's lentils here, or a bowl of cabbage soup at home.'

'Cabbage soup?'

'My mother's diet plan.'

'Your mother's a dietician?' he asked.

'Well, no.' Just getting Natasha round dancing classes, voice lessons and auditions had been a full-time job. Her mother hadn't had time for a job. Hadn't had much time for anything but her talented offspring's showbusiness career. 'But apparently this is the very latest, absolutely guaranteed to get you thin in no time flat—' He held up a hand to stop her. 'What?'

'Throw it away,' he said, and handed her a menu. 'I recommend the pasta.'

'You do?' Dodie brightened. 'But what will I do with the soup? There's a gallon of the stuff.'

'I meant the soup. Put it on the compost heap.'

'I don't have a compost heap. I don't even have

a garden. Just a courtyard with a few tubs of daf-
fodils and some window boxes.'

'Very low-maintenance.'

'Just the way I like it.'

'Gardening is excellent exercise,' he pointed out.

'It also gives you calluses on your hands.' Then,
'Forget gardening. My mother was chopping and
cooking half the night. She told me so. And think
of the waste. All the starving people—'

'If your conscience hurts, send a cheque. Getting
fit requires stamina, and you won't get that from a
bowl of cabbage soup.'

Stamina? She didn't like the sound of that. And
she didn't want to get fit; she wanted to get thin.
But for once she kept her big mouth shut.

'If your mother gives you a hard time, refer her
to me.'

The thought of the irresistible force of her mother
meeting the rock that was Brad Morgan distracted
her from the worrying issue of stamina and she
grinned.

'Now, that,' she said, 'I'd buy tickets to see.'

He responded with a lazy smile that lifted the corners of his eyes into a ripple of creases that held not
the slightest hint of mockery. And her stomach flut-
tered back in the most ridiculous manner, stopping
any desire for laughter in its tracks.

'Pasta it is, then,' she said quickly, handing him
back the menu. 'After which you might want to summon half a dozen strong men to carry me to my van.'

CHAPTER FOUR

'OKAY. This is the deal. If you're going to get toned up in time for that final dress-fitting you're going to have to work out at least every other day. As for diet—' he tapped the booklet on the table between them '—this will tell you all you need to know about sensible eating.'

'Thanks,' Dodie said dryly, 'but, having lived with Gina for three years, I do know all the rules for sensible eating. I just don't obey them.'

'Who does? But it's just for a few weeks. Fulfilling dreams requires at least some effort.'

'I walked ten miles today. That's effort.'

'You staggered a little over two miles.'

She felt like pulling a face, but decided against it. She needed Brad Morgan a lot more than he needed her. So what else was new?

'It's worth a little sacrifice to fit into the designer dress and attract the passing attention of the man of your dreams, surely? You can indulge in all the junk food you want when you get back to reality. The day after the wedding.'

She didn't like his tone. She didn't like it one little bit. He couldn't have made it clearer that he thought she was shallow and just a little bit stupid if she thought Charles Gray would look at her twice.

Hardly worth *his* effort, in fact.

Well, tough. He was stuck with her.

She put on a bright smile. 'You're right, Brad. I'll be sustained by the thought that I can hit the supermarket shelves the minute the wedding is over.'

His own smile was noticeable only by its absence as he said, 'What time is best for you?'

'Time?'

'For gym sessions. Are you free during the day, or does your work mean you can only come in first thing, or in the evening?'

'My time is my own, but I prefer first thing.' Once she'd started work she hated any interruption. 'Eight o'clock?'

Brad's look suggested that wasn't his idea of first thing.

'Seven, then?' she offered, suppressing a shudder.

'Okay. We'll start on light weights tomorrow. Eat a proper breakfast. Wholegrain cereal. Half-fat milk. A poached egg.'

'And no cabbage soup,' she said, trying, without success, to tempt out his elusive smile. Just as an experiment. To see if the stomach flutter was merely hunger.

'You can eat it if you feel you have to,' he said, without visible sign of amusement. 'But only after you've eaten the cereal and poached egg. If I even suspect you're messing about with the latest crash diet fad,' he warned, 'you're on your own.' He looked as if he'd welcome the excuse, but he was interrupted by one of the receptionists before he could say so. 'What is it, Lucy?'

'Maintenance have been looking for you, Brad.

There's a leak in one of the bathrooms over at the hotel and you—'

'I'll be right there.'

'You moonlight as a plumber?' Dodie asked, when the girl had gone. Then, because she couldn't resist, 'Or are you a plumber moonlighting as a personal trainer?'

He looked as if he was about to say something fairly caustic, but he took a deep breath and said, 'Me? I'm just your regular, all-round man-about-the-gym.' He got to his feet. 'Here comes your lunch. Enjoy it.' He told the waitress to charge the food to an account number—presumably hers—and apologised to the girl for not having time to stop and eat his.

He didn't apologise to her, Dodie noticed.

'Any instructions for dinner?' she asked, delaying his departure. He might be irritating, but she still wished he was staying to eat with her.

'Chicken without the skin. A jacket potato, no butter. Salad.'

'That's more than I eat when I'm not on a diet.' Of course she still ate all the bad stuff.

'It's *what* you eat that matters, Dodie, not how much. I'll see you tomorrow.'

She watched him as he walked quickly away. Forget Charles Gray. That man had the sexiest backside of any personal trainer-stroke plumber she'd ever met.

Brad checked out the leak in one of the hotel bathrooms and a couple of other maintenance problems.

Nothing major, but since he still had Dodie's camera tucked into his pants pocket he used it to take pictures to show the contractor, then left the maintenance crew to deal with them.

That done, he went to his suite, ordered a sandwich from the kitchen then, while he waited for his laptop to boot up so that he could download the photographs, he called Gina, planning to leave a message on her voicemail. She answered the phone.

'Good grief, shouldn't you be asleep?'

'Probably. Unfortunately my body clock doesn't seem to have worked that out. I was just going to call you.'

'No problems?'

'Everything went like clockwork. A very charming man was waiting to whisk me to the hotel, and the plan is for me to act like a tourist until Monday, by which time I should have adjusted to the time difference.'

'Make the most of it. Enjoy yourself while you're there. I don't just want great ideas, I want you full of energy and eager to implement them on your return.'

'Thanks, I will. Any problems at Lake Spa?'

'Nothing to worry you. Angie's in hospital. Appendicitis. I've sent flowers.'

'Poor thing!' Then, 'Oh, bother!'

'Don't worry about Dodie Layton. I've sorted that out.'

'Have you? I was going to clear that with you before I left, but you weren't in your office. You didn't mind me waiving the fees? I'm sure we've got the best of the bargain—although I have to admit I'd pay them myself just to see Dodie taking exercise.'

'She's a good friend?'

'The best. From first day at nursery school.'

'Well, relax. She's in good hands. I'm taking care of her myself.' There was a moment of stunned silence. 'Is that a problem?'

'Er, no. Absolutely not. I'm just surprised that you'd take on something like that. You must have a lot more pressing demands on your time.'

'Not that many. I leave the day-to-day running of the company to the clever people I employ for the purpose.' A fact she'd find out for herself if she lived up to her promise. 'And this seems the obvious solution under the circumstances—discretion being a necessity. The wedding is big news, and with the principle players keeping their heads down any story will be welcome. At least this way I can be sure her exercise programme won't find its way into the tabloids.'

'Oh, I see. You've worked out who she is.'

'I guessed when she told me she wanted to slim down for a big wedding. More specifically for the best man—'

'She told you *that*?'

'I think I might have made her just a little bit cross.' He found himself smiling as he remembered the quick flush to her cheeks. 'I suspect she said more than she intended.'

'That'll do it every time,' she said. 'Cross, she can be quite a handful. I'm really grateful you've taken her on. Dodie deserves a break, but it'll take patience to see her through—' A yawn caught her out. 'Sorry. Are you staying at Lake Spa all the time I'm away?'

'My secretary suggested I could do with a change,' he said, as she yawned again.

'I think my body has finally realised that something's wrong. What was I saying?'

'Something about patience?'

'Oh, right. I warned Angie that Dodie's a comfort eater—big time—and I suspect, for all her excitement, she'll find the stress of being her sister's bridesmaid hard to cope with.'

'You mean she'll be in the nearest pizza parlour the minute I'm out of sight?'

'She won't be able to help herself. She'll need watching.'

'I've noticed. So far she's lied about her weight, her height and her age.'

'And you called her on it? I bet she loves you.'

'Let's say we've reached a state of mutual understanding. I understand that she has a problem with numbers. She understands that I wasn't born yesterday. But I have rescued her from some nightmare diet of her mother's devising, so I think we're about even.'

'Her mother…'

'Yes?'

'Means well. Probably.'

'Three of the most damning words in the English language. Is there anything else I should know?

Anything that you might have told Angie personally rather than commit to paper?'

There was a pause. 'You seem to be taking this very seriously.'

'I take everything I do seriously. So?' he insisted.

'No. It's nothing. Really.'

He waited patiently while she weighed the benefit to her friend against betraying a sacred trust.

'Okay,' she said, coming down on the side of the benefit. 'When Dodie asked me to help her with this she said I was the only person who knew her well enough to keep her on track. That I'd go through her cottage and throw out anything that resembled temptation.'

'I can do that. It's not a problem.'

'It is, unless you know Dodie very well. She's like a squirrel. She tucks little treats away in case of an emergency attack of the blues. She's always needed the prop of comfort food—that's an old story—but it's got a lot worse in the last year, and once she started working at home the weight just crept on. The way it does.'

Home?

'You're telling me that she works from home?' he said, recalling the way she'd wriggled when he'd insisted that she walk to work. As if he was giving her a really hard time. And the way she'd made a major thing about capitulation. As if he'd won a really tough victory.

'Just for the last twelve months or so. Since she stopped teaching. It was painful at the time—a two-chocolate-bar-a-night crisis—but it hasn't all been downhill. She's been able to concentrate on her own design work. She's really exceptional. All she needs is to find some self-respect. To be able to look at herself in the mirror and like what she sees…'

Yes, well, he could sympathise with that. He knew what it was to look in the mirror and hate his reflection.

'When the standard is Natasha Layton, it's always going to be tough,' she said.

'Not that tough. They're different. Natasha Layton is the embodiment of the untouchable princess. The product of perfect make-up and lighting.' Never letting herself relax, even for a minute, in case the fantasy is shown up for what it is. He'd made a life's work of such women. 'It must take half her life just maintaining the image,' he said.

'And not just *her* life,' Gina muttered.

'Sorry?'

'Nothing. Look, Dodie uses a converted stable block at the back of her cottage, but don't be distracted by the resemblance to Aladdin's cave. You'll find an emergency supply of chocolate biscuits in a big jar in the corner, a packet of mints in desk drawer, a bag of—' He struggled with a desire to laugh. And lost. 'Okay, so she's a challenge,' Gina said, a touch uncertainly.

'Something I've never been able to resist. So what else was Angie going to do?'

It was her turn to laugh and she didn't make any attempt to stop herself.

'Did I say something funny?'

'No. Nothing. At least…' Then, 'You asked me

how seriously you should take Dodie. Just how serious are you prepared to be?'

Ten minutes later, he tossed the phone on the desk and downloaded the pictures from Dodie's camera. There were some fine shots of the complex taken from the dock. Her camera wasn't just a toy, he could see. She knew what she was doing.

Then he clicked onto the ones he'd taken of Dodie, her face pink with exertion, damp strands of hair clinging to her forehead and cheeks, a perfect example of ''before''. She'd stretched out their brief respite, insisting on taking more pictures of the lake, the Spa buildings on the opposite shore for 'inspiration'. As he flicked through them he found his thoughts straying to the way she'd felt as he held her.

Soft, voluptuous, womanly.

Hers was a body built for an earlier age—as curvaceous and well-upholstered as the much-loved vintage nineteen-fifties Jaguar on which his father lavished so much car wax and elbow grease.

Dated and desperately in need of a tune-up if the state she'd been in by the time they'd arrived back at the health club was anything to judge by. But still capable of making his heart beat a little faster than it had for some time.

With pure aggravation.

Despite her exertions, or maybe because of the additional oxygen whizzing around her brain, Dodie arrived home eager for work. She was still working at her computer, putting the final touches to the last panel of a commission she was working on, when a rap at the studio door jolted her out of her concentration.

She hit 'save', holding the image she was working on and, her heart sinking, she opened the door, expecting to see her mother on the doorstep, flushed and excited—the way she'd been that morning—with the latest instalment of the arrangements for the wedding of the year tucked under her arm. And another consignment of soup.

It wasn't her mother. It was Brad. Filling the doorway with his wide shoulders. His almost-smile.

It had to be relief that had her heart bounding skyward.

'I rang the doorbell, but there was no answer and I wondered if you might still be working. I hope I haven't disturbed you.'

His hope was unfulfilled. The Spring March sunshine had long gone. It was dark and there was a mist of rain in his hair and over the shoulders of his soft leather jacket. It sparkled softly in the light spilling out from her workshop.

She was a lot more disturbed than was sensible.

'I…um…' Her throat seemed momentarily unable to cope with anything as simple as conversation, so she lifted her wrist to check the time. She wasn't wearing her watch.

'It's nearly seven o'clock,' he said helpfully.

She flicked a stray curl behind her ear—she had to do something with that dangling hand—cleared her throat twice, and said, 'I'd no idea it was so late.

When I'm working I tend to forget the time.' Then, 'You'd better come in before you get soaked.'

'Thanks.'

He stepped over the threshold and suddenly her studio seemed small, cluttered with tubs of scrap cloth. Ribbons and sequins and braids. Utterly frivolous and almost painfully bright in contrast with Brad. He'd been impressive in grey sweats, but dressed entirely in black he was awesome.

'Would you like some tea?' she said. Well, she had to say something, and he didn't seem inclined to start a conversation. 'I keep a kettle in here for...'

'For emergencies?' The almost-smile deepened slightly and two strong lines bracketed his mouth. 'Sounds good,' he said, looking around, his gaze alighting on a series of richly embroidered panels pegged up out of harm's way until they could be stretched on a frame. Lush, rich, heavily embroidered, yet sharply modern.

'Wild flowers,' she said, before he asked. 'I've been commissioned to make a series of panels by a professor at the School of Botany. For his wife. She grows them,' she added, saying too much in an attempt to fill the silence. She indicated the computer screen. 'I'm still working on winter.'

'Snowdrops,' he said. 'Winter is black and white.'

Like him, she thought. Monochrome. 'Green, too,' she said, touching the frost-rimed grass, tracing it, her finger lingering on a shrivelled berry. 'And the tiniest touch of red.' Then, turning abruptly away, 'Milk? Sugar?'

'No, thanks. I wouldn't say no to a biscuit,

though. It's been a long day and, as you know, I missed lunch.'

She had her hand in the big terracotta jar before she realised what she'd done. 'Oh, right. Very funny. Gina's been checking up on me. Telling tales.' She turned to face him. 'Own up. You're here to frisk me for chocolate.' She put her tin of chocolate finger biscuits on the table beside the mugs and held out her hands, as if for cuffs. 'It's a fair cop, guv. I'll come quietly.'

He ignored her hands and instead opened the tin, took out a biscuit and bit it in two, which she thought was twisting the knife a little. Blushing a little at her boldness, she let her hands drop. Despite her equality speech that morning, she wasn't the kind of woman who could look a man in the eye and tell him what she wanted. She'd never had that kind of confidence.

'Actually,' he said, 'I came to return your camera.' He finished the biscuit, took her camera from his jacket pocket and set it beside her computer. 'In case you need it for work. I'm sorry I couldn't get here earlier, but I had a few things I needed to see to. And then I had to pack.'

'Pack?' She picked up her own mug of tea and took a mouthful. It was nearly cold, but she had to do something to cover the flutter of anxiety. It hadn't taken him long to change his mind about whittling her down to size. 'Where are you going?'

'Gina said you wanted Angie to move in with you, keep you on a short leash.' He helped himself to another biscuit. 'You should have told me this morning. I would have been here sooner.'

She spluttered violently and the tea took the short route down her nose, making speech of any kind out of question. He passed her a handily placed box of tissues and she grabbed one, mopping up the mess before blowing her nose.

'Okay now?'

Okay? Was the man mad?

'Sooner?' She didn't want to ask the question foremost in her brain. But she couldn't help it. 'You mean you're planning on moving in here? With me?' That needed more than cold tea, and she grabbed a chocolate biscuit a fraction of a second before he moved the tin out of her reach.

He caught her wrist, trapping it in long, hard fingers and removed the biscuit from her hand before she could get it to her mouth. Then he dropped it into her mug.

She let slip a word that shocked her. Brad did the gentlemanly thing and ignored it.

'Gina said you have a spare room in the cottage. I won't get in your way. In fact you won't even know I'm here—'

'You won't be here,' she snapped.

'—unless you decide to make a bacon sandwich in the middle of the night. In which case you'll find that I'm a very light sleeper.'

'I don't have any bacon.'

'You won't have when I've been through your fridge,' he agreed.

'But—'

'This was your idea,' he pointed out.

'My idea was that Gina should move in with me for a few weeks. I've known her—'

'Since nursery school. I know.'

Her chest was rising and falling much too quickly, her heart beating much too fast. It was understandable. She was furious. With Gina and with Brad Morgan. Standing there, looking as if butter wouldn't melt in his mouth.

'And she made it quite clear that Angie wouldn't be able to do that. She has a family—'

'Then you're lucky you've got me instead. I'm completely unattached.'

She swallowed.

'Gina said to give her a call if you have any problems.' He took a card from inside his jacket pocket and handed it to her. It was warm from his body and, disconcertingly, she felt an urge to rub it against her cheek... 'That's her number. She's probably awake by now. Or she should be if she's planning on having lunch.'

'You think I'm bothered about waking her up?' she demanded, finally finding her voice. 'She might be your boss, but she doesn't scare me. I knew her before she could do up her own buttons. Let me tell you, it would give me enormous pleasure to disturb her peaceful slumber...'

Realising that she was not behaving in a cool and rational manner, she stopped, picked up her mobile and punched in the number on the card. As it began to ring, she lifted her brows.

'This isn't going to be pretty,' she said. 'I'd rather not have an audience.'

'No secrets between a woman and her personal trainer, Dodie,' he said, and, having picked up the biscuit tin, he opened the top drawer of her desk and removed the bag of mints she kept there, pushing them into his pocket.

There was something about being so slickly out-manoeuvred that brought out the competitor in her.

'Okay, you've got me,' she said, with a you're-too-clever-for-me smile, and, taking the cottage keys from her pocket, offered them to him. 'You've cleaned me out in here. Do your worst in the cottage before you leave.'

She needed to shop anyway. She would take a nice healthy walk to the corner shop and replace it all after he'd gone.

He took the keys. 'I'll get my bag,' he said, which wasn't what she'd invited him to do at all. 'And I'll come back for the chocolate buttons in the…um… button box later. When you've finished your call.'

He closed the door behind him so smartly that the kick she aimed at it just missed. She might have taken another shot at it, but the phone was picked up at the other end and a bleary voice said, 'Hello?'

'Wake up, Gina. You've got some explaining to do.'

'Whoa, whoa. Time out.' There was thirty seconds of silence. 'Okay. I remember who I am now. Who are you?'

'Cut it out, Gina. Who is Brad Morgan and why does he think he can move in with me?'

'He's there already? He didn't waste much time.'

'Don't try and avoid the question. Why is he moving into my spare room even as we speak?'

'He is? Golly. Well, the thing is—and don't get angry with me because I haven't had much sleep in the last thirty-six hours—I did mention that you'd wanted me to move in and keep you on the straight and narrow. He thought it was a good idea, since he'd worked out for himself that you're not over-endowed with will-power.'

'He doesn't know that!'

'No?'

'You told him, didn't you?'

'I have your best interests at heart, okay? You're not giving him a hard time, are you?' she asked, anxiously. 'You do know how lucky you are that he's prepared to give you so much of his time?'

'Lucky? Excuse me? At this moment a man who is a complete stranger to me—'

Well, not that much of a stranger, since he'd taken a tape measure to her most vital statistics and was the only person in the world who knew the circumference of her thigh. She really hadn't wanted to know.

'Yes?'

There was something in Gina's tone that warned her to be careful about giving too many details.

'A man,' she continued firmly, 'who is at this moment clearing my kitchen of all the most perfect foodstuffs known to mankind—'

'A man dedicated to saving you from yourself, Dodie. You called me, remember? You wanted live-in help. Well, you've got it.'

'I wanted you! We're friends. We understand one another.'

'Which is why it wouldn't have worked. I'd have been out buying chocolate for both of us within twenty-four hours.'

'Gina, he's a man!'

'I had noticed. I'm glad you have. I was beginning to wonder if you'd forgotten they existed.'

'No chance. And he's not staying.'

'Before you do anything that you're going to regret—that I'm going to regret—I want you to listen to me very carefully. I have just four words to say to you, Dodie Layton.'

'Four?'

'Charles Gray.'

'Oh, right. Fantasy man.' She tried to recapture the excitement she'd felt when her mother had first called and told her about the wedding. About Charles Gray. She hadn't given him a serious thought since she'd fallen into the arms of Brad Morgan.

'And?' she prompted, preferring not to think about what that might mean.

'Martin Jackson.'

'Oh, that was below the belt.'

'You were the one who wanted this. I promise you, Brad knows how important this is to you—'

'You haven't told him about Martin? About what he did?'

Living with the fact that you'd been made a fool of by a man was bad enough. It wasn't a secret she was willing to share with anyone but her best friend.

'Relax. He knows nothing except that you want to get fit for your sister's wedding. And for the lovely Charles Gray. I didn't tell him that,' she pointed out quickly. 'You did. He's going the extra mile as a personal favour to me.'

'And of course the extra money for unsocial hours helps.'

'What?'

'Well, he's not doing it for love, is he?' Then, 'Are you okay? That sounds like a nasty cough.'

'It's just a dry throat,' Gina said quickly. 'The long flight, I expect. It's nothing that some undisturbed sleep won't put right. In the meantime, I'm not prepared to comment on the financial arrangements I've made with Brad. I promise you I won't be billing you for his time.'

'Too right, you won't. It isn't going to happen. What would you say if I suggested *you* let some strange man move into your spare room?'

'If he looked liked Brad Morgan I'd ask how soon he could move in. I really don't understand your problem. As I recall, we shared flats and houses with some very strange men while we were at uni, and had very little choice in the matter. Most of them were housetrained.'

Dodie's response was less than enthusiastic. In fact it was little more than a grunt.

'Okay, I'll admit I wouldn't want any of them camping out on my best sheets, but Brad Morgan is not some wet behind the ears undergraduate who needs his mother to show him how to wash a plate. He's out of a different league altogether.'

'Yes, but which one?'

'The premier division, I promise. You've got nothing to worry about with him under your roof.'

'You sound very certain. Is there something you aren't telling me?'

'Like what?'

'Have you given him a test run?'

'Oh, puh-lease. Workplace relationships are a recipe for disaster—' She stopped abruptly and Dodie didn't need to be in the same room to know that Gina had just stuffed her fist in her mouth. 'I'm sorry, Dodie, I wasn't thinking.'

'No problem,' she said, brushing the gaffe aside. The last thing she wanted was her best friend tiptoeing around her, afraid of hurting her feelings. Especially when she was trying to help. And getting a hard time for it. Maybe that was why, in the end, she capitulated without more fuss. 'I suppose it's not such a bad idea. He's no Charles Gray, but then who is?' she said, reminding herself just why she was doing this. 'And while he's here he could make himself useful. I could do with new washers on the bathroom taps.'

'Washers?' Gina appeared momentarily lost for words. 'Er, right. Well, no harm in asking, I suppose. After all, he's there to make all your dreams come true.'

'Looking good while dancing with a film star who won't remember me the next day? Giving my ex a bad moment over his morning paper? What kind of a person does that make me?'

'Human?'

'Too right. A human who could do with some new dreams.' It wasn't only her body that needed tuning up.

'Then why don't you do it just for yourself, Dodie? It's time to get what you want out of life.' A series of bleeps from the phone distracted her. 'Uh-oh. Sounds like your moby is about to go flat. Give Brad a chance and you won't regret it, I promise you—'

The phone cut out, leaving Dodie listening to silence. 'Do it for myself?' She looked at the phone.

Now there was a novelty.

Unwilling to go across to the cottage, she downloaded the photographs from the camera, looking at the ones Brad had taken of her, hot, sweaty and desperately pink in the face. She'd better do it for someone, she decided as she printed off an A4 glossy of the least flattering picture to put in a prominent position on the fridge door. And soon.

Still she delayed. Switching off her computer. Rinsing out the dirty mugs. Tidying up. Ignoring the hammering of her heart.

She was right about one thing. He was nothing like Charles Gray. Brad Morgan was real, if a bit battered about at the edges. He wasn't some make-believe figure of perfection who, if the truth was known, had facials and spent more time at the hairdresser than she did.

She was beginning to wish she'd never opened

her mouth and said the words 'Charles Gray' to
Gina.

To anyone.

Which was why, on the point of finally calling it
a night and locking up, she backtracked to collect
one last item before putting her head down and running through the rain to the cottage.

CHAPTER FIVE

DODIE burst through the back door, shaking rain-drops from her soft, light brown hair, stopping as she saw him leaning back against the kitchen table.

'Finished already?' she said.

'I've finished in here. I thought I'd better leave the rest of the house until you were here to witness fair play.'

'What a gentleman,' she said, but not with any conviction. 'At least I've saved you a trip back out to the studio in the rain.' And she dropped an un-opened packet of chocolate buttons onto the table.

Brad glanced at it, making damn sure he kept any inclination to smile under tight control. It was nicely done, but he recognised the feint for what it was. An attempt to keep him from making his own search of the studio. Gina had warned him that, whatever she surrendered, she'd hold something in reserve for a black moment.

Instead, he said, 'I appreciate that. How was Gina?'

'Cross.' Dodie, fixing the photograph to the fridge door with some magnets, glanced back at him. 'She didn't appreciate being woken up. And she wasn't best pleased with me for giving you a hard time.'

'Oh?' He wondered what exactly she'd told Dodie about him.

'She told me in no uncertain terms that I'm lucky you're prepared to help me.' Suddenly she was looking anywhere but at him. 'That I should stop whining and be grateful.'

'It's always good to be appreciated,' he agreed. 'But it's not essential. Just as long as you do as I say, I can live without you liking me.'

'Good. Did you find the spare room?'

'Top of the stairs. Door on the right.'

'It's a bit basic, I'm afraid.'

The whole cottage was very simple. White walls, black beams, uncluttered surfaces. The only splash of colour came from purple irises in a plain, brushed steel vase placed on an old pine kitchen table. Even her bedroom bore few traces of feminine occupation. Just the subtlest scent of Dodie Layton. As if she'd just walked from the room.

He hadn't gone in there, just opened the door, looking for somewhere to dump his bag. And for a moment he'd been captured by the contradiction between the woman and her surroundings.

'When I'm not working I need a rest from...' she made a vague gesture in the direction of the studio '...all that.'

'It's...calm,' he said. Unexpected.

'Calm?' That brought a wry twist to her mouth, a slanting glance in his direction. 'That's an adjective rarely used in conjunction with my name.' Then, with her gaze fixed upon the cardboard box he'd brought in from his car, and which was now filled with the contents of her fridge and store cupboard,

'I see you came prepared to clean me out. What are you going to do with all that?'

'That's not your problem.'

'No?'

And finally she turned those huge, dark eyes on him. The effect was like a punch in the stomach.

Unexpected was right.

'No. It's mine. I'll get it out of here right now.'

'Maybe you'd like to give a little thought about supper at the same time. Since the cupboard is now bare.'

'It's all in hand,' he managed, after a moment during which he struggled for breath. 'The chef at the Lake Spa restaurant prepared something simple. It's in the oven, heating through.'

Her mouth, which had betrayed tension, her unease at his presence, softened, and a dimple made a fleeting appearance, so brief that he might have imagined it. But hadn't.

'You know, Gina might be right about having you about the house.'

'Oh? What did she say?'

'Nothing much. Just that you were here to make all my dreams come true.'

'I'm afraid she exaggerated. My task is to give you an even chance of making your own dreams come true.' Then, because he wasn't entirely thrilled with her dreams, he changed the subject. 'Tomorrow we'll shop, refill your fridge with a more appropriate selection of food and then you can do the cooking.'

As if that effectively dealt with any nonsense about dreams.

'You *can* cook?' he asked. 'You don't just send out for pizza when you run out of chocolate biscuits?'

'Noooo,' she said, stretching out the vowel as she laughed at the very idea. 'Well, not more than three times a week.' Before he could say a word she held up a hand, palm facing him as if to fend off his wrath. 'Just kidding, okay?' Then, 'But if you're not going to do the whole new man bit, is there any chance that you might find time to fix the bathroom taps? You know, like a traditional old-fashioned man?' He had the feeling she was teasing, just a little, and that was unexpected too. 'You did say you were an old-fashioned man?'

Definitely teasing. Reminding him of his boast that he didn't kiss and tell.

He did kiss, though. And in the intimate confines of her small kitchen, with Dodie Layton no more than an arm's length away, he was sorely tempted to do just that. Reach out, take her into his arms and demonstrate that he was about as old-fashioned as it was possible for a man to get—for some weird reason she seemed to bring out the caveman in him—and a lot more real than some screen idol fantasy.

But he resisted. He knew how to keep his distance. He'd been doing it successfully for years. Mentally, if not physically. And that was where true distance was. Inside the head.

'What's the matter with your taps?' he asked abruptly.

'Nothing much. They just need new washers. My dad said he'd do it, but he hasn't found time. Mum

tends to keep him busy. Forget it if it's a bother.'
She said it casually. As if it didn't matter.

As if she was used to it not mattering.

'It's no bother. I'll sort it out tomorrow,' he said.
Then he picked up the groceries. 'Meanwhile, I'll
get rid of this.'

He carried the box outside, opened his 4 x 4 and
locked the box inside, out of harm's way. It was still
raining, but he was in no hurry to go back inside.
Instead he leaned back against the vehicle and lifted
his face to the sky, letting the rain wash over it, run
down his neck, chill his skin.

It wasn't working. The deeper heat that had
surged up in the closeness of the kitchen was turning
the rain to steam.

What on earth was the matter with him?

He didn't get hot under the skin for any woman.
He liked his relationships cool, contained, the kind
where everyone knew the boundaries. He dated
women who looked good on his arm, knew the score
in bed and never expected his heart to be included
with the trinkets that came gift-wrapped from some
fashionable jeweller's.

Women like Natasha Layton. Lovely to look at,
but whose self-obsession made it easy to walk away
without regret.

Dodie Layton was different. She was open, warm,
unconsciously sensuous. There was nothing con-
trived, no artifice in her appearance. It was all her.
Every soft, enticing handful. He just couldn't help
making the comparison with her sister. The fairy tale
against the reality.

Maybe he was being harsh. Maybe Natasha Layton was as lovely in her soul as she was in her body. But from one or two comments Gina had let slip he couldn't help feeling that what Dodie needed wasn't a diet at all, or even a get-fit regime.

That being suddenly admired, the centre of attention because she was thinner, had a new hairdo and a professional make-up job, wouldn't do her self-esteem any good at all.

It would simply reinforce all those feelings of inadequacy—her belief that image was more important than content—that made her reach for the chocolate in the first place.

'Brad?'

He straightened, turned his head as the light spilled out of the kitchen door onto the worn, wet cobbles and saw her looking out.

'Good grief, you're soaking,' she said. 'Come inside this minute and dry off before you catch pneumonia.'

'Yes, ma'am,' he said, straightening.

'Is it so bad?' she demanded, as he turned to face her.

'What?' he asked, as if he didn't know what she meant.

'Staying with me? You don't have to,' she said, 'if you'd rather not. I'll understand.' And she laughed, just to show it didn't matter one way or the other. 'I won't tell Gina, I promise.'

Somewhere deep inside, his well-honed self-preservation gene prompted him to grab her offer. Get out of there.

But he heard more than her intentionally careless laughter. He heard the defensiveness in her voice, heard her pushing him away first, before he walked away. Saw, in the light from the kitchen that haloed around her, glistened on her skin, giving it a golden glow, a contrary rigidity in her stance. It betrayed an expectation that he would grab her offer with relief.

That wasn't what surprised him. What surprised him was the realisation that she hoped he would.

And for once in his life he wished he'd taken a holiday.

He might have been bored, but he sure as hell wouldn't be totally confused.

For a moment he was seized with a quite alien desire to hold her, tell her that chiselled cheekbones were not the most important thing in the world. That she was lovely just the way she was.

He got a grip and used the fall-back plan that Gina had suggested in anticipation of this moment. 'Look, I know this is probably the last thing in the world you want, but to be honest you're the one doing me a favour. I could stay in the staff quarters at the club until I find a place of my own. They're not bad...'

In fact they were pretty damn fine, but he shrugged, suggesting quite the opposite, and tried not to regret too much the loss of his comfortable suite, his deck with its lakeside view and morning sunrise, the promise of sailing at dawn with nothing but the ducks for company.

The twenty-four service at the end of a telephone. 'A bit basic, but not bad,' he repeated. Then he grinned at her. 'But your cottage is a lot more comfortable.'

She'd be a lot more convinced by this evidence of his self-serving nature than by his unexpected response to her vulnerability.

'So why are we standing out here in the rain?' she demanded. Not entirely convinced.

'Now, I'm glad you asked me that,' he said, reverting to a serious expression. 'I've been standing here trying to work out how many times you'd have to cross the courtyard between the cottage and the studio to constitute a decent walk to work. Every day.'

'Oh...' Even in the uncertain light he could see that she'd blushed crimson. 'Sugar.'

'I thought much the same thing,' he admitted, 'when I realised that you'd been having a little joke with me.'

'I'm sorry about that. I really must try to keep my sense of humour under lock and key.'

'Don't do that. I enjoy a joke as much as the next man.'

'You don't have to be kind.'

'I promise you, I'm not,' he said.

'Oh.' Then, 'Did you, um, come to any conclusion?' And with an elegant little gesture she wordlessly indicated the distance between her back door and the studio. There was something about her hands. The economy of movement coupled with a grace that was totally distracting.

'Yes,' he said, crossing to the door and walking into the kitchen as she fell back to let him through.

'And?' she demanded.

She'd laid the table with some vivid hand-made crockery, put the salad he'd left in the fridge in a matching bowl, and a couple of dinner plates to warm over the cooker.

The kitchen was warm, bright, invitingly filled with the scent of good food.

'And you're right,' he said, reaching up to pull his shirt over his head. 'I'm wet.' He rubbed it over his hair, around his neck and over his arms. 'And starving.' He bent and opened the door to the washing machine and stuffed the shirt inside. 'Why don't you dish up? I'll be right back.'

Dodie, rooted to the floor, stared at the space so recently occupied by her unexpected guest. Had that really happened? Was she hallucinating, or had Brad Morgan just stripped off his shirt in her kitchen? Exposed the kind of shoulders and chest that would have lesser men stampeding for the gym and lustful women stampeding for the bedroom?

Her imagination, bless it, had suggested a certain drool-worthy element to his physique when she'd first set eyes on him. Her imagination, she discovered, was out of practice.

Nothing…nobody…no *body*…not even in her life classes, had prepared her for the reality of those long, elegant muscles. The small scars that her imagination, now on full alert and working overtime, suggested were the result of a collision of studded boots with living flesh. The spatter of hair which arrowed down in a fine dark line that would bisect his hips…

She swallowed. Blinked. Swallowed again. Then started as she heard movement in the room above her, his feet on the stairs.

Swinging around, she reached for a thick cloth and opened the cooker door. And when, as he ducked below the lintel of the doorway, she turned with the casserole between her hands, she prayed that her flushed cheeks would appear to be the result of nothing more disturbing than a close encounter with a hot oven.

'Did you find a towel?' she asked, without looking at him. 'I should have said. There are plenty in the airing cupboard. It's the last door...'

'I found one,' he assured her. 'There weren't that many places to look.'

'I suppose not. Well, just make yourself at home.' As if he hadn't already done that without any encouragement from her. Stripping off in the kitchen...

She picked up the serving spoon and offered it to him, but he fastened his hand around her own and she finally looked up. He'd changed his trousers—she supposed she should be grateful he hadn't taken those off in her kitchen, too—and was now wearing age-softened denims and a faded blue sweatshirt.

His damp hair was clumped in spikes, his chin shadowed with the day's growth of beard. He looked, sitting at her table, comfortably at home. As if he belonged.

'Did I embarrass you just now?' he asked, breaking into her mind-wandering. 'Break some house rule about getting naked in the kitchen?'

'No. Not at all.' Her voice was stiff, her body was

stiff and she felt terminally stupid. He must think she was behaving like an outraged spinster aunt. An outraged *virgin* spinster aunt.

On the contrary, her reaction was anything but outraged. She'd just been made mouth-dryingly aware of the barrenness of her life during the last year.

There were some things that neither hard work nor chocolate were ever going to replace. No matter how fiercely you closed your mind to them.

'It's just when you live on your own...'

When you lived on your own it was easy to forget the quick rush of desire. The low heat curling around your belly and thighs. Forget the comfort of waking up snuggled against another human being. Even if that human being turned out to be less your average *Homo sapiens* and more the order of mammal commonly known as *Rattus*.

'I won't do it again,' he said.

'Oh, no! Please!'

And the flush came rushing back to her face with no hot oven as convenient alibi.

'I mean...' She sat down rather heavily. 'Actually I don't know what I mean. I think I'd better just shut up now, before I make a complete prat of myself.'

He released her hand, took the spoon and, taking her plate, began to serve her with chicken breast and thinly sliced mushrooms in a tomato and onion sauce.

'Do you want to get the potatoes?' he suggested. 'Or shall I?'

She leapt up again, banging her knee on the leg

of the table. She didn't even notice the pain as she took the dish of small new potatoes, cooked in their jackets, from the warming oven and placed it on the table.

'This is nice,' she said brightly, as he put her plate in front of her. 'Maybe we should forget cooking. Maybe you could just bring home food from the health club every evening.'

'Not more than three times a week, surely?'

Her head snapped up, but he was smiling. 'Relax, Dodie,' he said, helping himself to chicken, then potatoes. 'Tell me about your work. Gina mentioned that you used to teach.'

'Oh?' Her heart began to hammer against her ribcage. 'What did she say?'

'Nothing about your job. Just that you'd started to put on weight when you weren't dashing to the university every morning.' He glanced at her. 'Which apparently coincided with a sudden escalation in your chocolate habit. What happened?'

His glance became something deeper as he held her gaze.

'Happened?' she repeated, playing for time and at least some semblance of coherent thought to extract her from this weird longing to tell him the whole hideous story.

'Why did you leave? Clearly you were upset, or you wouldn't have needed wholesale quantities of chocolate.'

'I only did that once!' she declared hotly. 'I was going to the cash and carry anyway. Gina had no right—'

She stopped, horrified. Closed her mouth so fast that her teeth snapped together. She'd got her distraction, the rapid change of subject that she'd been desperate for. Unfortunately she'd made a complete fool of herself into the bargain.

In the silence of the kitchen the sound of her clearing her throat was painfully loud.

'Gina didn't tell you about that, did she? About the time I bought a whole carton of chocolate bars? The ones with raisins and caramel and pieces of biscuit. And a box of Easter eggs.' Right after she'd walked out of her job and the only way to blot out the pain had been to just keep eating.

She'd probably have eaten the lot if Gina hadn't arrived in the nick of time and rescued her from death by chocolate.

'No,' he said. 'It must have slipped her mind.'

He'd better not laugh. He'd just better not laugh, that was all.

He didn't.

What he did was get up and look in the fridge. And when he turned back, with a small bottle in his hand, his face was straight enough. Unfortunately there was a telltale twitch at the corner of his eyes to betray the trouble he was having keeping it that way.

'Would you like some of this dressing on your salad?' he asked, and covered his mouth as he gave a little cough. She wasn't fooled for a minute. 'It's low fat.'

'Then what's the point?' she said, more to be contrary than because she didn't believe it would be good.

'Try it and see.'

She shrugged, speared a mushroom and ate it, while he poured on the dressing, mixed the salad, spooned a pile onto her side plate. Then, 'In answer to your question, I left my post at the university to further my career as a designer. It was a risk,' she said. 'Stressful.' She cleared her throat again. 'Hence the chocolate.'

'But now you're an independent artist with a growing demand for your work?'

'Yes. An independent artist with a growing demand for my work and a burgeoning backside because I don't walk to work every day.'

There was more to it than that, Brad thought as they ate. It explained the lack of simple exercise that had once been slotted so seamlessly into her working day that it had been quite painless.

But he didn't buy the stress. Anyone with the guts to go it alone didn't need that kind of prop.

There had been something else that precipitated the change. Something so bad that she'd rather make herself look foolish than talk about it.

'We'll fix the backside,' he promised as he put down his fork.

'We?' She brightened a little at that.

'Sure. I'll tell you what to do. You'll do it,' he said, cruelly slapping down the answering cheer that seeped through him.

She looked as if he'd slapped her. He didn't have time to dwell on any feelings of guilt, however, because the phone rang, rescuing them both, and she leapt up to grab it from its wall mounting next to the fridge as if it were a lifeline.

She was barely half way through her name before she was interrupted.

'Mum—' she said. 'How are—?'

Interrupted for the second time, she glanced at him and unnecessarily mouthed the words *my mother* at him.

'Soup?' She pulled back her lips against her teeth in a rigor of panic. 'Absolutely… Yes… No… I can see how… No, really, it's wonderful. I feel thinner already…' And she patted her backside as if her mother could see. 'No, really, there's no need… I can make it and you must be so busy…'

There was a long pause during which she was clearly being given chapter and verse on exactly how much organising a wedding entailed and during which the occasional 'goodness' and 'amazing' and 'poor you' from Dodie were all that was needed. He had the feeling she'd had a lot of practice at this.

He pointed at her plate, wordlessly asking if she'd finished.

She nodded and he began to clear away.

Leave that, she mouthed. *I'll do it.* Then, 'What appointment?' she yelped, startled out of her semi-attention to her mother. 'What dress designer?' Her eyes widened in horror as her mother repeated what she'd said. 'Yes, amazing…' But she was shaking her head and silently mouthing, *No, no, no…*

'Isn't it a little bit soon? I need some time to whittle off…' There was another long silence while she

listened. Then, despairingly, 'Well, if it's just an initial look to see what might suit me I suppose it
would be all right. Nine o'clock…'

He crossed to her, covered the mouthpiece and
said, 'I have precedence over dress designers.
You're mine until ten o'clock.'

Then he released it, but leaned against the wall,
keeping close in case she needed a second reminder.

She glanced at him nervously. Mouthed, *But I
have to go!* She looked desperate, but he wasn't letting her off the hook. She didn't have time to play
hooky. The designer was going to have to work
around him.

'The backside comes first,' he murmured.

She swallowed. 'Look, Mum, I really can't leave
here until ten o'clock. I've got an…um—' She
glanced at him for help.

'Meeting?'

'Meeting,' she said, grabbing his suggestion with
a quick smile of gratitude. Then, 'Who with?'

Good grief, her mother didn't give up easily.

'No one you know,' she said. Then, 'Of course
it's important!'

There was another long burst of words that rattled
like a machine gun against Dodie's ear if the way
she held the receiver away from it was anything to
judge by.

'Yes, Mum. I understand that the wedding is far
more important than anything I could possibly…
Yes, I know it has to be perfect for Natasha… Of
course I want to be her bridesmaid. She's my sister—'

'Ten o'clock,' he repeated firmly as he sensed her wavering under this onslaught.

She threw him a look of desperation, then, 'No! There's no one here... You must be able to hear the radio... Look, give me the designer's telephone number and I'll give him a call. I'm sure we can sort out a time that suits us both.' She grabbed a marker pen that was attached to the fridge and wrote a number on the door. 'No! Really! There's no need to come round to explain the soup plan again. I've got it sorted. Just concentrate on Natasha.'

She hung up the receiver and leaned back against the fridge door, breathing as heavily as if she'd just run a mile. 'That was intense.'

'If I hadn't been here you would have caved in.'

'Probably,' she admitted. 'But only because being measured for a designer dress is marginally less painful than anything you've got in store for me.'

'Thank you for the ''marginally''. Coffee?'

'Please.'

He crossed to switch on the kettle, and spooned some coffee into the cafetière. 'It's a pity you didn't get the whole rebellion over and done with and tell her what you did with the soup.'

'I didn't do anything with it. Oh, I see. You mean that I didn't...um...eat it.'

'No, I mean the bit about flushing it down the toilet.'

'In my dreams,' she said. 'Besides, it would be lying.'

'And letting her think you're eating the foul stuff is telling the truth?' She at least had the grace to look sheepish. 'Besides, you might not have done it, but it was the first thing I did when I cleaned out the fridge. Didn't you notice it was gone?'

'I was too busy pining for the good things you chucked out,' she admitted. 'I suppose I should thank you for small mercies.'

'My pleasure. But, forgive me, I don't understand your squeamishness with the truth. You were quite shameless about telling her that there was no one with you.'

'That wasn't a lie. She meant with as in "with".' She used those pretty hands to sketch the quote marks. 'In the sense of *please* let her be with someone before she ends up an old maid, left on the shelf.'

'Old maid?' he said. He grinned. 'Aren't they supposed to be virgins?' he said, and got the pretty blush again.

'I was speaking figuratively,' she said.

'Of course. Old-fashioned sort of woman, is she? Your mother.'

'Not old-fashioned, exactly. She just doesn't have much faith in my ability to support myself. As an artist.'

'You seem to be doing well enough. A charming cottage. Commissions lining up.'

'I rent the cottage,' she said. 'And I blew my big chance of a good, steady husband—a man with prospects and a pension plan. She isn't over it, which is why I don't want any misunderstandings about you.'

She finally looked up at him, taking in his appearance, his favourite jeans and sweatshirt so old that wearing them had to be rationed to extend their lives.

'Not that I imagine she'd confuse you with either good or steady,' she said. 'But it might be better if you didn't answer the phone when I'm not here. Not until the answering machine's clicked in and you know it's safe.'

'Forgive me, but aren't you a bit old to be worrying what your mother thinks?'

She grinned. 'You should wait until you've met my mother before you go asking damn fool questions like that.' She spun as there was a rap on the door. 'Good grief, she's here.' Dodie looked at him, then at the dishes piled in the sink, with pure panic in her eyes. 'She does that,' she says. 'Rings up and then, if she thinks you're not listening properly, comes round and says it all again.'

'You're twenty-seven years old, Dodie.'

She opened her mouth to say something, but instead frowned. 'How do you know that?'

'Because Gina is twenty-seven. Twenty-eight next month. I was giving you the benefit of the doubt.'

'I think I might just hate you.'

'Give it time. If you don't now, you will.' The rap at the door was repeated. 'Are you going to answer that? Or shall I?'

She straightened, ran her hands through her hair as if it would make the slightest bit of difference to her appearance, and then crossed to the door, taking a big breath before she opened it.

But it wasn't her mother. It was a man. Well groomed, expensively dressed in a cashmere overcoat.

'Martin.'

She'd taken a big breath, but his name still came out in that kind of knocked-out voice that happens when you run out of air with excitement or shock. Brad couldn't see her face, so he couldn't say whether she was out-of-breath excited, or out-of-breath shocked. Or whether the two things were the same.

CHAPTER SIX

'AREN'T you going to ask me in, Dodie?'

She'd imagined this moment so many times in sugar-fuelled daydreams. The knock on the door. Martin Jackson standing on her doorstep. Sorry. Begging her to forgive him. Grovelling for her to take him back.

She'd run the whole gamut of responses. There was the one where she was dignified and gentle as she gave him a chance to explain himself. A bit of a fantasy that one.

Then there was the you-must-be-joking rage of a woman who had been cheated on by a man she trusted. An ear-ringing response that would have him running for his life.

And shamefully, in her lowest moments, there was the one where she just flung herself into his arms and dragged him to bed before he could change his mind. The nightmare scenario.

'It's raining out here,' he prompted, with a brief gesture that took in a coat that must have cost far more than even a Senior College Administrator could afford. But Martin had never been short of money for the really important things. A good hair-cut, the right clothes.

'Sorry,' she said, shaking herself. 'You're the last

person in the world I expected to see on my door-step. What do you want?'

Then, as his head lifted, stilled, she didn't need the hand on her left shoulder to know that Brad was standing behind her, like a bulwark against harm.

'Is there a problem?' he asked. Then, 'You'd better come in. You're getting drowned out there.' She'd probably imagined the reassuring squeeze as he eased her gently back, but his hand never left her shoulder even when, as Martin responded to his invitation and stepped over the threshold, he extended the other. 'I'm Brad Morgan.'

Martin, smooth as oiled silk, scarcely missed a beat as he took in the scene of domesticity in a single glance. He slipped the buttons on his overcoat and then smiled. 'Martin Jackson,' he said, taking Brad's hand in the briefest of acknowledgements. 'Dodie and I used to work together. Among other things.'

'What do you want, Martin?' she repeated.

'That coffee smells good. I've just come from work.'

'Change your job,' Brad advised. The man glanced at him as if he were crazy. 'No? Well, in that case take a seat. I'll get another cup.'

Dodie felt a tiny spark of pleasure as Martin, eyes momentarily narrowed, watched Brad demonstrate his total familiarity with her cupboards—he had spent the last hour clearing every nook and cranny of hidden treats—as he reached, without searching, for another cup, implying, no matter how unintentionally, that he was at home here.

She'd spent the last year reliving every moment

she and Martin had spent together, analysing every gesture, every expression. Trying to work out what she'd missed, what she'd done wrong. And she discovered now she could read this look without the need for an interpreter.

He wasn't happy finding another man in what he still considered his territory.

It would have been gratifying, amusing, even, if it hadn't been so hideously painful. Martin had never been able to find a cup or a spoon in her kitchen. But then she'd been so pathetically grateful that he'd loved her that she'd never expected him to do anything as tedious as make her a cup of coffee.

Maybe that was why it hadn't occurred to him that she might not be on her own. Having seen the morning papers, the news of Natasha's wedding, and decided that the opportunity for networking would more than make up for a little grovelling in an effort to make his peace with her, it hadn't occurred to him that he might actually have some competition.

'You've changed the cottage,' he said, looking around at the white walls, the Shaker simplicity of the furniture. 'Is every room as spartan as this?'

'Spartan?'

'Minimalist, then.' He smiled. 'Is that the correct word?'

'I just got rid of the clutter.' She sat down quickly as her legs began to quiver. 'The dust-catchers.' Anything that didn't earn its place by being either useful or beautiful. Anything that wasn't totally honest.

'Even that silk canopy over the bed? The one made from an old sari?'

She felt her face heating up. Not with embarrassment that he should imply such intimacy, but with anger. 'An antique sari,' she corrected, keeping her voice even, keeping her hands out of sight beneath the table so that he shouldn't see them shaking.

Not looking at Brad.

'Milk, Martin?' Brad said, placing a cup of black coffee in front of him. A small jug. 'I'm afraid we don't have any sugar.'

'No sugar? No cream?' Martin ignored Brad and looked directly at Dodie, as if to remind her of the voluptuous pleasures they had shared in the days when it had been her pleasure to cook for him. His pleasure to be served. 'I can't believe you've changed that much.'

Believe it and weep, she wanted to say. But then he'd know that it was him she'd been sweeping out of her life. Everything he'd touched. Everything his breath had touched.

She'd scrubbed her own skin until it was raw.

She didn't want him to know he'd been that important. That he'd hurt her that much.

Seeing him look pointedly at the unflattering photograph pinned to the fridge door, the one that suggested the change had been very recent, she repeated the question.

'What do you want, Martin?'

'Me? Nothing. I'm here on official business. From the university.' He glanced at Brad, as if hoping he'd take the hint and go away. Instead he leaned back against the deep butler's sink, cup in hand. Martin shrugged, poured some milk into his coffee. 'As you must have heard, we're hosting the Armstrong Lectures this year.'

'The Armstrong Lectures?' Brad repeated, refusing to be ignored.

Martin held Dodie's gaze for a moment longer before, with a tiny smile that suggested they were part of an inner circle to which Brad could never belong, he turned to answer. 'A series of lectures sponsored by the Armstrong Media Group which is based here in Melchester. They're a major platform for new ideas in the field of popular culture. Television, sport, that sort of thing. I'm surprised you haven't heard of them.' He sipped his coffee. 'This is good,' he said, and smiled at Brad. 'I've never quite got the hang of making it myself.'

'It isn't difficult. Like all good things, it just requires time and effort.'

'Well, I'm a busy man,' he said dismissively, as if the simple task of making good coffee was beneath him.

Dodie held her breath, but Brad simply smiled as Martin turned back to face her with a patronising shrug. Of course, he was a master of the smile. This one might have fooled Martin, but it wouldn't fool her. It never left the surface.

Martin reached out, put his hand on her shoulder, distracting her. 'Time, as you know, Dodie, is the one thing I don't have—'

'So?' Brad interrupted, giving her an opportunity to pull away without making too much of it, ease back in her chair, putting some distance between them. 'What have they got to do with Dodie? The lectures?'

Martin drew in a breath, fighting down his irritation at another interruption and not quite succeeding. 'This year the theme is Art in the Twenty-first Century,' he said, without bothering to turn and look at Brad. 'New materials, new techniques. Dodie is an acknowledged expert in the use of computers in the field of textile design. We were very sorry to lose her,' he said, as if willing her to read more into his words, 'although of course we understand that her own artistic career has to come first. I don't have to tell you, Dodie,' he said quickly, before either of them could interrupt him again, 'that there's a list of artists as long as your arm who would kill for the opportunity to give one of these lectures.'

'I wouldn't name any of them,' she said, impatient for him to get to the point and leave. 'It would be slander.'

He brushed her interjection aside with an impatient little gesture. 'I believe I can persuade the Vice-Chancellor to put your name at the top of the list. I want you to give the first lecture.'

'When is it?' Brad asked.

Which was just as well, because her mouth had suddenly dried. This was the last thing she'd expected, even when Martin had brought up the subject. She'd assumed he was going to invite her to the reception afterwards as his guest. Bridge-building time. But this—

An Armstrong Lecture would propel her name

into the spotlight. It would mean features in the arts pages in the national newspapers. Colour spreads in the weekend supplements.

The kind of exposure that, with luck and a following wind, would make her as well known in her own field as her sister was in the theatre.

'It's next month. What do you say, Dodie? Will you do it?'

'That's very short notice.' Brad's voice cut in with a warning note. 'Dodie's extremely busy for the next few weeks.'

'With Natasha's wedding? I saw the story in the newspaper this morning. To be honest—and call me cynical, if you must—that's why I want you to give the lecture. It'll be a really big opportunity to raise your profile. And of course it'll be good for the college, too.'

'I'd have thought your speakers would have been booked months ago. Did someone drop out?' she asked.

He smiled, held up his hands. 'You're too clever for me, Dodie. I admit, we've had a speaker drop out, but I'm sure you're not going to stand on your dignity and throw the opportunity away. Be grown-up about this. Give the lecture and we'll all come up smelling of roses.' He gave a little shrug, a gesture that suggested he knew what she was thinking. 'You believe it would be tacky to use your sister's wedding to advance your own career?'

She didn't want to be grown up. She wanted to be very childish and tell him exactly what to do with his lecture.

But before she could begin to frame the words, he said, 'Do you think Natasha would think twice if the boot was on the other foot?'

He already knew the answer to that one, Dodie thought. He knew all the answers. He'd probably invented some of the questions.

'I owe you, Dodie. We both know that. I hoped this offer might draw a line under all that.' He looked for a moment as if he was going to say more, but instead he got to his feet. 'I'll leave you to think about it.'

'I don't—' She caught Brad's warning look and something made her stop herself from saying that she didn't need any time to think. The answer was no. No matter how good it was for her career she didn't want anything to do with it, not if it meant being in the same room as him. 'I don't know what to say.'

'Why don't you talk it over with your mother? She's a clever woman, ambitious for her children. I'm sure she'll understand how important this is for you. But don't leave it too long.' He glanced at Brad. 'Thanks again for the coffee,' he said, then, standing on the doorstep as he buttoned his coat, asked, 'Is that your 4 x 4?'

'It belongs to my company,' he said.

Martin smiled as he walked across to a brandnew sports car. 'You'll get a letter from the Dean about the lecture in the next week or two, Dodie. Give me a call. We'll have lunch.'

For a long moment after she'd shut the door the kitchen seemed to ring with silence.

'That was him,' Brad said finally. 'The chocolate man.'

'You've got him pegged,' she said, and laughed, but not with humour. The sound was harsh and painful even to her own ears. 'Martin Jackson. Smooth, sweet and good to look at.'

'He's not a teacher, surely?'

She shook her head. 'He's the Art Department's administrator. Finance, staffing…'

'It must pay well. That coat didn't come off the peg in the high street.'

'He has a good eye for a picture. Recognises what's going to catch the eye. Buys cheaply from students who need help with their overdrafts. Sells when they make their name.' She shrugged. 'And they always do seem to make their name. They adore him.'

She picked up her cup and swallowed the coffee. Black, unsweetened, it took some swallowing. She didn't want sugarless black coffee. Her mouth craved chocolate, as her body had once yearned for Martin Jackson. Both equally bad for her.

'I thought he'd come to weasel an invitation to Nat's wedding,' she said. 'He always did manage to surprise me.'

She tried not to think about the chocolate buttons locked away in Brad's car. Or the biscuits. Kept her fingers so tightly around the cup that it was a wonder it didn't break.

'Will you do it?'

'Do what?' She dragged her mind back to the kitchen. To Brad. 'Oh, the lecture.'

She shrugged, embarrassed at how much she wanted to do it. Angry with herself that, even knowing how important it was, she'd been prepared to throw it back in Martin's face.

It had been a year and still she was allowing his betrayal to hurt her. Hurt her career.

'I'd be a fool not to,' she said, finally answering Brad's question. 'I might hate the fact that he's the one giving me the chance, but I don't need my mother to point out the facts of life to me. This is what it will take to get commissions to do the big, important pieces to hang in public buildings.'

She put down the cup and scrambled quickly to her feet, not looking at him. Afraid to meet those penetrating blue eyes head on, to let him see how much the idea of being grateful to Martin Jackson was tearing at her.

'Look, I really need to get back to work. Those panels have to be ready by the end of next week.' She gestured towards the washing up, the cluttered table. 'Leave all this. I'll get it later.'

She didn't wait for him to answer her, but wrenched open the kitchen door and dashed across the courtyard, fishing the keys out of her pocket as she ran. She unlocked the door with shaking hands, practically falling through it in her desperation for something, anything, to block out memory.

She didn't stop to put on the light—she knew every inch of the studio and knew exactly where to look. She reached for the handle and pulled out the bottom drawer of her desk without so much as a fumble. It was right at the back. It had to be there.

She groped frantically and then her fingers fastened around the chocolate equivalent of a life jacket.

Only to be used in the most desperate of circumstances.

She took it out, then curled up on the floor with her back against the wall, ignoring the chill as she tore off the wrapping. It was the finest chocolate. Dark. Seventy per cent cocoa solids. There was nothing to beat it for a quick chocolate high, and she momentarily allowed the scent of it to engulf her in the dizzying pleasure of anticipation before she snapped off a square, put it in her mouth.

For a moment it lay there, crisp and cool against her tongue. Then, as it reached body temperature, it melted like silk and, with a groan of pleasure, she closed her eyes.

Standing in the darkness of the studio, Brad heard the snap of chocolate. He could have stopped her. He probably should have stopped her. Because he'd known, even before she left the kitchen, that she was running for her emergency back-up supplies.

She'd been outwardly calm with Martin Jackson, but he'd seen the effort it had taken to keep herself from reacting to his presence. The tension as her fingers had worked pleats into the cloth of her cargo pants beneath the table.

Unfortunately he hadn't been able to decide if she wanted to kill him, or to throw herself at him. Just because someone had behaved badly—and he was certain that Jackson had behaved very badly indeed—it didn't mean you stopped wanting them.

The only thing he'd been sure of was his own reaction. Regret that he'd pressured Dodie into inviting him in. Her shock, confusion, as she'd confronted the man had left him in no doubt that this was the man who had caused all the trouble in the first place.

But it had seemed too good a chance for her to clear the emotional decks the way she had cleared her home of his presence. Once she was sure how she felt about Jackson it would make his own job easier.

So much for playing amateur psychologist.

Nothing was ever that simple. Certainly not Martin Jackson. He hadn't been there two minutes before he'd starting jerking her strings. Drawing her back to him with his offer of a prized lecture.

Brad wondered if that had been his initial intention. Or if his own unexpected presence had forced the man to change tack, try just a little bit harder.

It shouldn't be that difficult to find out. All he had to do was give Mike Armstrong a call.

As for his own very real desire to pick Martin Jackson up and fling him bodily out again into the rain… Well, he'd like to put that down to the man's patronising remarks about his 'good' coffee, the implication that Jackson was, himself, far too important to find the time to make his own.

And by implication Brad wasn't. Important. Or busy.

Jerk.

Unfortunately he couldn't put it down to anything of the kind. He didn't need anyone to bolster his ego. He knew who he was. What he was. It had been a tough lesson, hard-learned. But he had learned it.

No. His anger, cold, hard and bolted firmly down where it could do no harm, was purely the result of the way the man had looked at Dodie. Touched her hand. As if he'd owned her once and could do so again. All he had to do was click his fingers and she'd fall right into line.

Maybe he was right.

He was dangling a great big carrot, inviting her to bite. And she would bite. She'd be a fool not to. After that it would be just a question of one step at a time until she was right back into his arms. At least Brad had stopped her from doing it there and then. At least he'd made the bastard sweat a little before he got what he wanted.

But it was her choice, he told himself, ignoring the sharp stab of something very like jealousy that knifed through him. He would have to stand back and let her decide whether to kick the jerk or kiss him.

What he wouldn't do was stand back and let him drive her into a sugar overload. He was prepared to concede one square of chocolate. She'd had a shock. But as a second snap, loud as a pistol-shot in the darkness of the studio, warned him that she wasn't going to stop at one, he covered the distance from the door, reached down and caught her hand before she could lift it to her mouth.

'Enough,' he said sharply, taking the bar from her other hand, tossing it over his shoulder through the open doorway.

Dodie had been so lost in her anticipation of sensory gratification that he'd taken her completely by surprise, and she jumped as if scalded at the sound of his voice. The touch of his hand.

'Brad! I didn't hear you—'

Then, as he lifted her hand—and with it the chocolate—out of reach, she forgot what she was saying. Instead she howled with frustration, and, coming up onto her knees, followed the hand with her mouth.

'Stop that!' he said sharply, pulling it back.

Since she was still holding the chocolate he couldn't let her go, but as she used her other hand to make a grab for it he caught that too, gripping her with both wrists, holding the one with the chocolate at full stretch so that she couldn't get to it.

And just for a moment she seemed to collect herself. Laughed.

'Oh, look at me,' she said. 'What am I like? I just don't know what came over me.'

'I understand. It's okay. Look, come on. Up you get—'

Even as he relaxed his guard, loosened his grip on her wrist to take her elbow and help her to her feet, she made another wild lunge, taking him off balance so that the back of his knee hit something hard and buckled beneath him. He went down, cursing, but he was damned if he was going to let her have it now. And with her wrist still clamped tightly in his hand she had nowhere to go—except crash down on top of him.

Completely lost to sense, she made another grab to reclaim her prize, wrestling with him the darkness, her full, lovely breasts soft against his chest, her scent mingling with that of the chocolate.

Going down for the second time, this time drowning in a riptide of sensual heat, he made a determined effort to regain control, capturing her free arm, pinning her hard against him in an attempt to make her stop thrashing about before chocolate became a secondary problem.

For a moment they lay perfectly still, her hand imprisoned in his fingers and at full stretch above his head. The only sound was their commingled breath, snatched in short gasps as they recovered.

Still—he discovered belatedly—was not necessarily *safer*. Just a different kind of danger.

Still, the pressure of her body against his became more focused, more intense. And now he had time to notice the details.

Her hair shimmering in the faint light from the window. The soft touch of it against his face, his neck, trailing across his mouth. Huge dark eyes, darker even than the chocolate she craved. A full, pouting lower lip, invitingly soft, shining moistly, an invitation to touch, taste, share her passion, share her appetite. Her thigh pressed hard against his hip.

'Please, Brad,' she murmured, her voice soft as a baby's breath, pleading with him. 'I want…' she said breathlessly. 'I need…'

'What?' His own voice was thick, husky. 'What do you want, Dodie?'

Not chocolate, Dodie thought.

And, as if he knew, he eased the pressure on the

hand pinning her hard against him and slipped it beneath the hem of her T-shirt.

She held her breath, afraid that if she said anything, did anything, he would stop. And then he opened his fingers, spreading them across her back. His hand was hard, his thumb slightly rough against her skin as he began to move it in slow, sensuous circles down the deep groove of her spine. She tried to keep still, but his fingertips trailed against her ribs and she shivered.

'This?' he said. 'Is this what you want?'

He lifted his head, caught her lower lip between his teeth and, grazing it gently, teasing it with the tip of his tongue, tasted her, savouring her as he sucked it into his mouth. The pleasure of it spread heat through her limbs, a heavy languor to her abdomen and thighs.

She knew what he was doing, but he was doing it so well, and with a low sigh she responded, touching his upper lip with her tongue, running the tip slowly along the silky skin just inside his mouth.

Brad caught his breath on a moan of pure pleasure as Dodie returned his instinctive response to her need with a sweetness that left him defenceless. Without warning, the want was all his. A hot, hard ache that demanded attention. He slid his hand down to cradle her backside, press her hips into his so that she could be in no doubt that his appetite was every bit as urgent, every bit as basic as the one driving her.

'You're beautiful, Dodie,' he said, as he lifted her hand back over his head, loosening his tight grasp, kissing the backs of her fingers in a gesture of homage. Surrender.

'Beautiful?' He heard the soft choked sound as, painfully, she tried to laugh. 'Please...'

'Beautiful,' he insisted. 'Don't let anyone ever tell you otherwise.'

He heard a tiny sigh, a little mewl of pleasure, a soft, throaty laugh that went straight to his groin. Then, her voice a little shaky, she asked, 'Does that mean I can have the chocolate?'

'Sure,' he said.

The chocolate was soft and melting and, never taking his eyes off her face, he turned her hand and slowly, one at a time, he licked it off her fingers. Then he took her thumb into his mouth and sucked it clean. The chocolate was smooth, sensuous, but nothing like as addictive as the taste of her skin, the heat of her thumb lying against his tongue.

But finally he let her go, and, his voice cracking from the tight curb he'd placed on his own racketing desire, he lay back and said, 'You want it—take it, baby. It's yours.'

CHAPTER SEVEN

DODIE's limbs were liquid, her entire body on the point of dissolving with pleasure. It would be so easy to sup sweet victory from Brad Morgan's mouth, take her time about it...

Then taste the rest of him.

And after that get naked and invite him to return the compliment.

But while her body was zinging with excitement, urging her to go for it, her mind simply refused to let go, suspend disbelief. Instead it was standing back, rationalising the situation, pointing out that this must be something of an occupational hazard for personal trainers.

Needy women, low on self-esteem, suddenly the focus of attention from a man who was—well, in Brad Morgan's case anyway—sex on legs could so easily get the wrong idea. Mistake the 'personal', for something, well, *personal*.

When he was just doing his job.

Not that he appeared in any way reluctant to put in the overtime and go the extra mile to give her back her self-confidence. Ample evidence that he was ready for action was pressing hard against the worn cloth of his jeans. Against her thigh. Proof and to spare that he was not only willing but ready to make the ultimate sacrifice to save her from a chocolate binge.

For that she should be grateful.

Not on the point of tears.

But recognising the moves for what they were, knowing that she would just be another sad woman he'd eased through the pain, made it easier to call a halt, back off before it became something that meant he'd have to go. That she'd be thrown back onto her own resources. And the cabbage soup.

'Dodie?' His voice was a gentle query, and his hand against her skin, tender, caressing, halted her retreat. Both promised that this wasn't just part of the service. For a moment she allowed him to hold her. For a moment she wanted to believe him.

But that little voice of common sense yattering noisily away in the back of her head reminded her how much it would hurt when she discovered that she'd been fooling herself.

'It's okay, Brad,' she said, pushing herself away from him, sitting back on her knees. Away from temptation. She tried to ignore the fact that she was spread-eagled, in the most intimate manner, across his hips. 'I'm over it. You've proved your point.' She found a small, face-saving laugh from somewhere as she mentally urged her legs to support her so that she could stand up. 'Nicely done.'

'What point would that be?' he asked, his hand still lightly resting on her waist as if he would keep her there, not joining in with the laughter. Had she got it wrong? Had that kiss, his caress—?

She stopped the thought before the voice of com-

mon sense was drowned out by something much
more earthy, primitive; it was already fading, harder
to hear. In a desperate attempt to regain control of
the situation she reached out as if for assistance and
her hand met the leg of her workbench. She grabbed
hold and hauled herself to her feet.

Her legs wobbled a bit. A small voice that wasn't
common sense told her that she was a fool to herself—as if that was news—but she managed a vague
gesture that suggested he knew exactly what she
meant. That there was no need to have a conference
on the subject.

For a man with a dodgy leg, Brad was fast. He
curled himself off the floor and was at her side before she could take another step, pinning her against
the bench—not physically, but with the sheer force
of his will—blocking her escape route to the door.

'What point would that be, Dodie?' he repeated,
with the kind of dangerous calm that warned her he
wasn't going anywhere until she told him what the
devil she was talking about.

Her body, confused by all the conflicting signals
it was getting, didn't want to go anywhere. It wanted
to stay this close to him. To feel the heat of his body,
his breath, just like this, against her cheek. It wanted
his arm around her.

It just wanted him.

Her mind, bless it, recognising the emergency,
scrambled to save her from herself. He'd asked, so
she'd tell him. If he didn't like her answer that was
his problem.

'Your point that I use chocolate—food—as a surrogate for sex,' she said, the words sounding as if she was talking from a distant planet. But once she'd said that, the rest was easier. She even managed a smile, although whether he could see it in the darkness was a moot point. 'Well, maybe I do. But, as you can see, I don't use sex as a substitute for chocolate. If you're staying, you're staying in the spare bedroom.'

She gathered herself, took a step forward, expecting him to back away and let her go. But he didn't budge an inch. He simply reached out, cradled her face in his long palm, the tip of his thumb brushing tenderly against her cheekbone, his fingertips resting lightly against her temple in a gesture that was nothing but comfort.

No, no, no! That was wrong. He was supposed to back off. He was supposed to be just a little bit hacked off, for Pete's sake, like any normal man who thought he'd hit pay dirt and then had the plug pulled at the last minute.

He wasn't supposed to be kind. He'd told her that he wasn't kind. But it seemed that he'd been lying about that, and it took all the will-power her mind could summon up to stop her body from simply leaning into the caress. Rubbing her cheek, like a kitten, against his palm.

'You're wrong, Dodie,' he said, and his voice was as gentle as his touch. 'I don't believe you're using food as a substitute for sex. If you were that easy to please, you wouldn't need chocolate.'

And he bent to kiss the top of her head—which for some stupid reason brought tears stinging to her eyes—before he let his hand fall to his side, turned abruptly and walked quickly from the studio.

She wanted to go after him, demand to know what he'd meant by that. Ask him why he was being so damned...*nice*!

Common sense suggested that she'd be much wiser to stay put and do what she'd said she was going to do. Get on with some work. It was a close call, but she'd made it, blinking back the tears, furious with herself for being so gullible as she wiped away one that had managed to escape.

Then she leaned over her desk, turned on her computer. The action made her feel better. She was in control there.

Leaving it to boot up, she flipped on a switch to flood the studio with light, banish the shadows. She glanced out into the courtyard, saw the bar of chocolate lying where Brad had tossed it. He'd apparently forgotten it, missed it in the dark. She wasn't tempted to rescue it, but instead closed the door on the rain and turned to lean back against it.

Her studio looked just the same as it had when she'd left it an hour or so earlier. Before she'd shared a meal with Brad. Before Martin's unexpected visit had sent her running for comfort.

So why did she feel so different?

Because Brad Morgan had kissed her? Touched her?

Oh, right. As if she was some naïve little virgin.

With a wordless exclamation of disgust, she crossed to the sink to rinse the residue of chocolate from her hands. Trying not to think about how Brad had licked them clean.

But, on the point of picking up the soap, she hesitated and instead lifted the tip of her thumb to her lips in curiosity—to taste Brad Morgan as he'd tasted her. And for a moment she had to clutch at the edge of the sink to steady herself, stop herself from crumpling to the floor as her body responded with an urgency, a hot desire that took her breath away.

Brad gripped the kitchen table with both hands, taking deep breaths. Damn! What was it about Dodie Layton that just made him want to reach out and touch? And keep touching.

Her hair hadn't been styled by some fashionable Knightsbridge crimper. She tied it back in the kind of band one of his little nieces might wear. She didn't use expensive cosmetics. Hell, she didn't use *any* cosmetics. As for her scent…forget anything that cost more by weight than gold. She smelt of nothing more exotic than fabric conditioner.

She was overweight, out of condition, and hadn't a clue how to make the best of herself.

She wasn't his kind of woman.

But her lips were creamy soft, her skin was silky beneath his touch, her body, lush and warm, overflowed invitingly into his arms and he wanted her the way he'd wanted no other woman in what had been an eternity.

He slapped the table with the flat of his hand. He didn't do this. He wasn't some callow boy to have his head turned by any woman. He'd been there, done that. Never again.

He was in control of his life.

He slumped into a chair, dragged his hands over his face, raked his fingers back through his hair. He *had* been in control of his life until Dodie Layton, walking backwards into trouble, had fallen right into his arms.

And now he was the one in trouble.

But that wasn't a problem. This was trouble he could walk away from. Hadn't those soft lips been telling him to get out of her life from the moment he'd invited her to sit down?

All he had to do was use the phone and he could have someone else getting her toned up for her date with Charles Gray. Turning her into the perfect bridesmaid.

Then, all he'd have to do was rid himself of the taste of her.

Forget the look in her eyes in that unguarded moment when all her feelings were laid bare—before she'd listened to the warning voice of experience and chosen the wiser course of discretion, preserving herself from the risk of further pain. Something he'd been doing successfully for years.

Until today.

Dodie stared at the screen, regarding the bones from which she planned to construct her winter panel with enforced concentration. Work was the answer. It had helped her through the terrible days, weeks, after she'd walked out of her job, her life. It would help her ignore the hammering desire, the hot little swirls of pleasure at the memory of Brad's kiss, his touch, his tongue sucking chocolate from her thumb in a manner so shockingly sensuous that just thinking about it made her weak.

She refused to be weak.

It would mean nothing to him. Absolutely nothing. She kept repeating that to herself as she stared at the screen, wondering why something that just a couple of hours ago had appeared to be the perfect composition of light and shade, a classic depiction of the cycle of nature, death and rebirth, now seemed just a tired cliché.

The frost was a schmaltzy, Christmas card touch. Winter wasn't pretty. Winter was rain, the endless sound of dripping water. And it didn't stop at the end of winter, she thought as a swirl of rain, heavier now, rattled against the window and her mind, let off the leash, instantly offered her the image of Brad standing in the doorway, his hair misted with it.

And her fingers began to race over the keyboard as she began to create something new, something fresh, completely lost to any sense of time, working until her eyes would take no more. But she was finally ready to start work on constructing the last panel first thing tomorrow—

No. She sat back, pinching at the corners of her eyes. Tomorrow she had a date with some weights. Had to phone the dress designer. Make a decision about the lecture. But not even the thought of talking to Martin again could spoil her mood.

She briefly touched the screen, then switched off. Stretched. She was tired, but pleasantly so.

She locked up, stooping to pick up the chocolate with its soggy wrapping as she ran across the courtyard, dropping it in the bin as she passed. Then she came abruptly to a halt and swung back round.

Brad's big 4 x 4 was no longer backed up neatly alongside her van.

For a moment she stood there, just staring at big empty space where it had been. Unable to quite take in what it meant. That he'd gone.

Not noticing the rain sluicing down the back of her neck, soaking her hair, running off her face.

Only wanting to tell him about the changes she'd made to the panel. An idea she'd had for the lecture. Eager for the warmth of her kitchen, where she'd imagined them sitting together at the table over a last cup of tea before bed, talking about what they'd be doing tomorrow.

Maybe she'd have asked him what he'd been doing before he started working at Lake Spa. What he wanted to do with the rest of his life.

Questions that had filtered between the cracks of her mind as she'd worked. One leading so naturally to another. Where had he come from? Did he have family? What did he like to eat at breakfast?

Now all she could feel was the cold pit of her stomach, hollow, empty, cheerless as the weather.

He hadn't even bothered to say goodbye.

She didn't know how long she'd been standing there, but she was soaked to the skin when she finally dragged herself to the cottage door, left on the latch so that just about anyone could walk in. She looked around. Everything was neat, tidy. As if he'd never been there. Except that he'd cleared her cupboards of anything that might cheer her up.

She pulled a face.

No. Forget that.

Right now, there wasn't a thing on earth that could make her feel better. Not even a jumbo-sized box of the finest handmade Belgian truffles. And she shivered, despite the warmth from the Aga.

A hot shower might stop her catching pneumonia, though.

She flipped up the latch on the door, kicked off her shoes and, doing what Brad had done earlier, stripped off her sweatshirt and cargo pants. As she opened the washing machine to toss them in, her mouth dried. Brad's shirt was still there, forgotten in his hurry to get away from her. Not just his shirt. There was a soaking wet tracksuit.

She reached out and touched it lightly. If he'd put it there, he must be—

A creak on the bottom stair warned her she was about to have company, and she yanked her hand back and leaped to her feet, spinning round as Brad stepped down into the kitchen, towelling his hair dry. Again.

'I see I needn't have worried about stripping off in the kitchen,' he said.

He was wearing a thick white bathrobe and quite probably nothing else, if his bare ankles and feet were anything to judge by.

'I—I thought you'd gone,' she said, her feet apparently superglued to the spot.

'Gone?'

'Your car...' she began. Then stopped, embarrassed, as she realised just how insulting the suggestion that he'd left without saying a word must appear.

'You thought I'd decided it wasn't worth my while staying over?'

She swallowed.

'If that's the way Martin Jackson treated you, Dodie, you need to mix with a better class of man.' Then, before she could even begin to frame an apology, 'I wanted to get rid of that box of food before the Camembert made the Jeep uninhabitable. I drove over to the health club and put it in the dumpster.'

'Wanted to make sure I didn't break into your car in the night, you mean. For a little midnight feast.' He didn't deny it. 'And?' she prompted.

'And, since I needed a run, I left it there.'

'At the health club? But it's...miles,' she said.

'Three, near enough. I looked through the window when I came back, but since you were still working I thought you wouldn't want me to disturb you.'

Too late. She appeared to have been disturbed beyond mending.

'Besides, I was steaming. A shower seemed like a much better idea.' He appeared to be struggling with a grin. 'You seem to have had the same one. I didn't use all the water.'

'Well, thank you for that.'

'No, Dodie, thank *you*.' And he lifted his brows

a fraction and let those blue eyes drift down her body in a manner that raised a blush and invited a slapped face.

Her fault, she supposed, for just standing there, indulging in polite conversation whilst wearing nothing but her underwear. While she acknowledged that stripping out of her wet things instead of trailing them through the cottage had to be the smart choice, she really, really wished she'd been stupid and gone straight upstairs and stripped off in the bathroom.

Of course she'd have walked in on him, but, while she'd still have blushed, he'd have been the one without any clothes on.

But she could handle it. It wasn't as if she was anything *like* naked. She wasn't even wearing any of that barely-there, scraps-of-lace kind of underwear. She kept the thongs and the oh-la-la stuff for occasions when it would be appreciated. Which meant it was right at the back of her flimsies drawer. Not wanted in this life.

Right now, she was kitted out in the kind of sensible stuff that stood up to the rigours of the regular cycle in the washing machine.

She shrugged. 'You said it, Brad. No secrets between a personal trainer and his client.'

'My recollection,' he said, 'is that you weren't wildly enthusiastic about the idea at the time.'

'Oh, for heaven's sake,' she said, finally managing to unglue her feet from the spot in front of the washing machine and head for the stairs. 'We're both adults—' As she moved, she caught sight of herself in the mirror situated conveniently by the back door. It wasn't fancy, but it was long enough to stop her leaving the house with her skirt tucked into her knickers.

If only.

The rain had soaked right through her clothes and her sensible underwear was clinging to her, damp and transparent. She wasn't naked. But she might as well have been.

At least fancy underwear would have focused attention away from the cellulite.

In these passion-dampers, she just looked…damp. And with a howl of anguish that Gina probably heard on the West Coast of America she fled for the stairs and the safety of the bathroom. It was possible that she might never come out again.

She should have been able to take a small crumb of comfort from the fact that now, at least, he wouldn't be interested in sharing her room, even if she had completely lost her head when he'd kissed her in the dark.

The light in the kitchen was totally unforgiving. It left nothing to the imagination.

But the bathroom was still warm, the mirror steamed, and as she turned on the shower, peeled off her wet underwear before stepping beneath its warm comfort, she was confronted with his shower gel hanging beside hers. And she couldn't stop herself from remembering that, just minutes earlier, he had been standing right where she was.

Far from comfort, she was left with the disturbing feeling that he was still there, with her.

The truly unsettling feeling was that she wished he were.

A sharp rap on her door at some unearthly hour before it was truly light dragged Dodie unwillingly from sleep.

She was never exactly lark-like first thing, though she could pretend if she had to. But she knew there was some special reason why she didn't want to get up today.

'Dodie!'

Brad Morgan. That was the reason. He was going to take her unwilling body and force it to do things that any sensible person knew was a bad idea.

'I've changed my mind,' she mumbled, then buried her head beneath her pillow.

Burying her head was a mistake, because the first indication she had that Brad wasn't taking no for an answer came when the warm cocoon of covers was whipped smartly back and she was left at the mercy of the March chill. She didn't need to sleep with her window open to benefit from good fresh air. The draft that blasted through the badly fitting old window was quite sufficient.

'Nice pyjamas,' he said, as he slowly scanned her fleecy PJs, the material having been chosen for warmth over style. 'There's something so, um, sexy about rabbits.'

She considered screaming, but decided it was too early. Instead she swung her legs off the bed and pushed her feet into a pair of furry rabbit slippers with floppy ears and whiskers. And a bob tail at the back.

Well, heck, a girl had to co-ordinate.

Another smile—the man had a whole wardrobe full of them. This was one she hadn't seen before, couldn't quite interpret. Amusement, certainly, but affectionate amusement? That seemed unlikely.

'You have no idea how cold this bedroom gets in the middle of winter,' she said defensively, before he could make any more smart comments.

'I have just the cure for that.'

Oh, right. That was original. Not.

'Warm-up exercises?' he offered, making her glad she hadn't said that out loud. At least she hoped she hadn't...

'Warming up for what?' she asked, thus demonstrating that while her eyes were open her brain was still in the Land of Nod.

'A bike!'

It was propped against the wall, a helmet resting on the saddle. Brad picked it up and handed it to her.

'You'll need this.'

She needed nothing except to wake up and discover this was a dream. One of a series that had disturbed her sleep. The kind where you're running naked. Only she hadn't been trying to run.

'Where did it come from?' she demanded, ignoring the helmet. 'And—' far more importantly '—where is my van?'

Because alongside the gap that had once contained his 4 x 4 there was now a smaller, but equally empty space: the one where her van lived when she wasn't using it.

Then, because she'd just taken the keys from the hook behind the door, had them in her hand, it occurred to her that she was being way too calm.

'It's been stolen…' she began, on a rising note of panic. 'Of all the—'

'No! No, it's okay; it's perfectly safe,' Brad cut in quickly. 'I borrowed it first thing—'

'It's "first thing" now!' she exploded, relief warring with fury.

'—to go and fetch the bike.'

'You mean you didn't *walk*?' she demanded. Sarcasm could become second nature if she was around Brad Morgan for too long. 'Or run?'

'I know I said you should walk everywhere,' he said, ignoring her outburst and using the kind of calm, reasonable voice that was guaranteed to make her completely lose it. 'But I don't think you're ready to walk as far as the health club yet. Not if you're going to be fit for any kind of workout when you get there.'

She gave up on the sarcasm and tried a little reason herself.

'This is a joke. You're kidding, right? Please tell me that you're kidding. I mean, you watched me take the keys…'

By way of answer he placed the helmet on her head, straightened it, then, apparently satisfied, bent to tighten the strap beneath her chin.

'You'll need your keys to drive home,' he said.

It was just cold that brought that nipple-tightening response from her body as his fingers brushed against her throat, she told herself. As he glanced up, his eyes on a level with hers. His mouth inches away from her own.

She was grateful for the heavy fleece-lined sweat-shirt that disguised it.

'Brad, I haven't been on a bike since I was...' She realised her mistake as the fan of fine white lines that framed his eyes disappeared in creases of amusement. And she said something rude.

'I'd have taken bets on you saying that you'd never ridden a bike in your life,' he said as he picked it up and turned it around, holding it in a silent invitation for her to get on.

'It's first thing,' she muttered, easing herself onto the saddle. 'My brain isn't awake yet.' And she'd been distracted by her hormones.

'Just close your eyes and think of Charles Gray,' he said, leaving his hand alongside hers on the handlebar, gripping the back of the saddle with the other, his whole body steadying her as if this really was her first time.

She turned to look at him, almost close enough to kiss. His lips would be cold, she thought. But his mouth would be hot.

'I, um, don't remember that bit in the Cycling Proficiency Test,' she said.

Now, if he said, *Don't worry, I'm right here. I won't let go...*

'Don't worry, I'm right here. I won't let go until I can see you're safe.'

Had she said that out loud?

'Do you want to give it a try?' he prompted.

'There's no way I can bribe you to call a taxi?'

'All you have to do is say stop. I'll go away and leave you alone,' he promised. He looked pretty confident that it wasn't going to happen.

'One of these days,' she said… Then she pushed off, wobbling around the courtyard a couple of times before, gathering confidence, she eased out into the road and headed for the cycle path that led to the lake.

Then, realising that she was on her own, that he didn't have a bike, she panicked, wobbled again. 'Brad!'

'I'm right behind you,' he said. She glanced back and saw that he was running smoothly and effortlessly just behind her. He looked amazing. Hard, fit and…

And she ran off the path, the thick dried grass at the edge bringing her to an abrupt stop. He caught her as the bike began to topple. Held her tight.

'Forget what I said about keeping your eyes closed,' he said, not quite so calm or reasonable, his heart pounding hard against her. Well, he'd been running.

'Right,' she said. 'You're the expert.'

'And perhaps in the interests of safety you'd better stop thinking about Charles Gray, too.'

'Who?' she said.

He thought she was joking.

CHAPTER EIGHT

'How's it going?' Since Gina was calling her from Los Angeles to check up on her progress, Dodie didn't waste time on niceties.

'If I tell you that I haven't eaten a cheeseburger since Brad Morgan moved in,' she replied, 'will that give you some idea of the suffering I'm having to endure?'

I'm impressed. How did he manage that?'

'By being pitiless. He's totally oblivious to a woman's needs.'

'Oblivious?' Gina seemed to find that funny. 'I suggest it's time for you to rethink what constitutes "a woman's needs". Get it right and I'm sure he could make you a lot happier than the world's biggest cheeseburger.'

'I wouldn't know about that,' she lied. He'd been more than willing to fulfil any needs she cared to name in that long, delicious moment when he'd licked the chocolate from her fingers. She must have made her feelings very plain, because he hadn't made the same mistake when he'd confiscated her triple-decker cheeseburger, the one with extra pickles.

She blushed as she recalled her lapse from grace. But after a totally healthy, totally good for her week, when she'd done everything Brad Morgan had demanded of her—even resisted the lure of the buffet car twice, when she'd taken the train to London to be measured and fitted for 'the dress'—something had finally snapped.

She'd felt hollow, empty. Comfort food had been the only answer.

And it was all Brad Morgan's fault.

After her wobble on the bike, he'd kept his distance. Gone out of his way not to touch. Kept his shirt on at all times. Restricted his early-morning calls to a sharp rap on the bedroom door as he passed.

Then, a week after she'd signed up to get fit, when it was time to weigh and measure, check her progress, and she'd been eagerly anticipating the moment when he'd get out his tape measure and slide it around her bosom, he'd made some excuse about a telephone call. Asked one of the girls to do it.

The harder she worked, the longer he occupied her spare room, the further he seemed to retreat from that moment of intimacy when, in the darkness of her studio, anything might have happened. When all she would have had to do was shut down her brain and let her body take over.

Her body had been giving her a hard time for not doing just that. It would keep *wanting*. And her brain was no help at all, with its vivid images of Brad stripped to the waist, of his eyes, dark and dangerous in that moment before he'd kissed her. She'd even begun fantasising about how it would feel to have his thumb brush across her mouth, his hands cupping her face, his body backing her up against the nearest obstacle until she stopped trying to escape, because there was no escape.

The further he retreated, the more intensely she yearned for him to come close. She'd become so sensitive to his presence that he only had to enter a room for the down on her skin to stir. If he'd touched her it would have been like an electric shock.

Maybe he knew it too.

Maybe that was why he'd asked someone else to do the business with the tape measure.

But he'd relented sufficiently to give her a ride home. Not that he'd been inclined to talk, and he'd been so deep in his own thoughts that she hadn't dared interrupt. If he'd talked to her she wouldn't have noticed the drive-thru' burger bar on the ring road.

'I'm going to change,' he'd said, following her into the cottage after he'd unloaded the bike from the back of the Jeep, heading immediately for the stairs so they wouldn't be crowded into the kitchen. Then, looking back at her from the safety of the stairs, 'If you want to put in some time in your studio,' he said, 'I can get supper.' Keeping them apart.

And that was when she snapped. When her comfort zone turned needy and began to whine.

If he wasn't prepared to offer her comfort—okay, so she'd told him she didn't do that, but she was entitled to change her mind, wasn't she?—she knew exactly where to get it.

'Thanks,' she said, her imagination—fuelled by the scent of frying onions—already working on the details of her breakout. She'd have her comfort and he would never know. 'All this exercise might be great for my body, but it's not doing much for my creative output.'

'Anything you'd like especially?' he asked.

'Anything but chicken?' she offered, willing him to just get on—go upstairs and change. But just when she wanted him to make himself scarce he seemed oddly reluctant to move. 'Or chicken. I don't mind,' she said, almost twitching at the thought of the warm calorie high that would be hers just the minute he took his eyes off her. A triple-decker cheeseburger. The infallible bulwark against emotional disturbances. Satisfaction guaranteed. 'I'll, um, get on, then,' she said, backing towards the door.

Still he didn't move, and she had to force herself to turn and walk, not run, to her studio. She switched on the lights and the computer, fumbling a little at the thought of the treat to come, muttering under her breath… 'Come on, come on…' Not at the computer, but at Brad, who seemed to be taking for ever.

Finally, after what seemed like an age, the light came on upstairs in the bathroom. She was finally free to grab the bike and make a mad dash for the drive-thru' on the ring road, rapping out her order as she skidded to a halt by the window.

'Fries with that? A drink? We've got a special deal—'

'No, thanks.' She didn't have time for the whole sales pitch, not if she was going to get back before Brad missed her. He'd looked…well, as if he could read her mind.

Impossible. If he could read her mind, she wouldn't need comfort food.

She paid, picked up the food and scooted through into the car park where, ignoring the cold, she sat at one of the picnic benches.

Eyes closed, and about to sink her teeth into the forbidden treat, she felt a prickle at the nape of her neck and knew that she was not alone.

She opened her eyes, looked at the burger in her hands. Then, with a sense of doom, she turned round.

'You are so predictable, Dodie,' Brad said, taking the burger from her hand. He returned it to its box and, ignoring her pitiful whimper, tossed it into the nearest bin.

'How did you *know*?' she demanded, almost gasping at the sudden withdrawal of her food fix.

'You were as taut as a guitar string this evening.'

'And you knew I'd head for comfort food heaven.'

'You sat up like a hungry pup when we passed this place earlier.'

'Just hungry,' she said. 'Desperate for—'

'You're not hungry,' he said. 'Not for food.' He stuffed his hands hard into his pockets, as if to stop himself from throttling her. Or something. 'You know, you've had a terrific week, Dodie.'

She swallowed. A terrific week. If he'd said that twenty minutes ago…

'I haven't lost any weight.'

'Forget your weight. You will lose weight but only if you keep going. You're walking taller, looking stronger, leaner. A week ago you couldn't have flung yourself onto a bike and raced over here to get your calorie fix.'

'A week ago,' she said, 'I didn't have a bike.' She wouldn't have needed one. She'd have had something handy in the fridge to assuage her need. Except that it wouldn't have satisfied it. Any more than the triple-decker would have given her what she wanted.

'You're not even out of breath,' Brad pointed out.

'Why did you have to say that? Now I don't just feel hungry, I feel *guilty*.'

'So you should. And I shouldn't have let you out of my sight. It's just as well I went over to the studio to see if you'd like to go out for dinner tonight.'

'Out? For dinner? On a diet?'

'It's stage two of my plan. A lesson in how to eat out without going into calorie overload.'

'Oh.'

'Exactly. There I was, full of good intentions. And there you were. Gone.'

'I needed…' she began, in an attempt to explain. She stopped. That was so lame. 'I wanted…'

'Yes?'

Him to notice her. Touch her. Go back to where they'd been that first night in the studio, before they'd both put up the barriers. She couldn't say that, so she said, 'I think I must be a really sad person, Brad.'

'Pathetic,' he agreed. Without a hint of a smile.

'I've let you down. I'm really sorry.' And she was. Not for the burger. But for messing up the opportunity to put on some make-up, dress up and spend the evening getting to know him in civilised surroundings. Instead of working up a sweat in the gym. 'After all your hard work you deserve better.'

'No, Dodie. After all *your* hard work *you* deserve better. You're not doing this for *me*.' She flinched at his all too genuine anger. 'Frankly, I think you look pretty amazing the way you are, burgers or no burgers, but my opinion doesn't count. Charles Gray is your target and, if the gossip pages are to be believed, he likes his women skin and bones.'

'But I'm not—'

'What?'

She'd been going to say that she wasn't going to all this effort to impress Charles Gray. But if she was really doing it for herself, that made the burger episode truly sad.

And if she was doing it to impress Brad Morgan? Pretty damn stupid.

'I'm not skin and bones,' she said.

'No.'

'Never will be.'

'It seems unlikely,' he agreed, far too readily, even if he was right. Then, 'I'm going home, Dodie.'

Her head came up. He was leaving? Just because of one tiny little incident with a cheeseburger? A cheeseburger that she hadn't even *tasted*. She didn't get a second chance?

'Shall I put the bike in the back of the Jeep?' he asked. 'Or can I trust you to cycle home on your own?'

Home. He meant *her* home! And a warm surge of

pleasure wiped out any lingering desire for the quick satisfaction of fast food.

'You can trust me,' she promised, shivering now she'd cooled off from her dash on the bike. 'But I'd rather ride home with you. Please.' Then, on an impulse, as he opened the door for her, as his hand beneath her elbow sent a heat wave of desire surging through her, she turned to face him, looked up at him with a boldness that shocked her even as she said, 'Do I get compensation? For the burger?' wondering what kind of kiss could adequately replace anything as totally satisfying as a triple-decker. Hoping that she'd find out.

'Compensation?' The word was little more than a murmur, but it reached right down inside her, stirring a longing so desperate that it scared her right back into her shell. 'What did you have in mind, Dodie?'

Before she could even begin to frame a response he reached up, touched her bottom lip with his thumb, leaned into her and followed it up with his tongue.

'This?'

He didn't wait for her answer—which was just as well since she was beyond coherent speech—but caught her upper lip between his teeth, teasing at it as he cupped her face in his hands and backed her against the cold metal of the sill. She grabbed at his shoulder to stop herself from falling back against the seat as the kiss deepened into something much more intense, bunching his shirt beneath her fingers as his thigh parted her legs, gripping as if she would never let go...

A loud whistle followed by raucous words of encouragement from some passing boys finally brought the kiss to a premature halt—any time in the next millennium would have been too soon. Gina had asked her, and Brad had asked her, what she really, really wanted. Now she knew. She wanted him.

'Does that cover your burger, Dodie?' he murmured, easing back but not letting go.

'Um, that's fine,' she said, swallowing hard, her skin seared by the heat that flared in his eyes. She'd been wrong about the electricity. This was something much more dangerous.

'Sure?'

'Absolutely…fine.' Then, because he didn't seem convinced, 'It was, um, on special offer.'

For a long moment he stayed exactly where he was, looking at her as if he wasn't about to let it go at that. Then he straightened, let his hands fall to his sides, and she edged back up into the seat without taking her eyes off him as he very gently closed the door between them. He took his own sweet time about stowing the bike, taking the opportunity to climb back from the brink of whatever precipice it was that they'd just teetered on.

When he slid behind the wheel he was back to his usual cool, distant self. While she felt like a limp rag.

She did a little deep breathing until she was sure she could match his emotional distance, then said, 'I suppose an invitation to dinner is out of the question after my fall from grace?' Well, someone had to break the silence. But she was careful to keep her eyes on the road ahead.

'Bread and water for you,' he said.

'That's not fair,' she protested. 'I didn't actually *eat* the burger.'

Out of the corner of her eye she saw his mouth lift in a wry smile. 'I suppose I could concede a point and make it breadsticks.' She said nothing, but her heart lifted an inch or two. 'And maybe a glass of red wine.'

'Without food? It would go straight to my head.' Then, pushing her luck a little further, 'We could take another turn around the drive-thru' and pick up something to eat,' she suggested, still not looking at him. 'If we had fries, we'd have all the major food groups.'

'It would be no more than you deserve if I took you at your word.' But the warmth in his voice re-assured her. He knew she was kidding. He was kidding, too. 'Have you tried that Italian restaurant near the cathedral?'

Startled out of her composure, she glanced at him. 'I can't afford to eat in places like that.' She left unsaid the thought that he couldn't either. She had the feeling it would be a mistake to say it out loud. Maybe, if it was a lesson in eating out without blowing the calorie account for a month, he planned to get Gina to pay it out of expenses. She should be shocked, but she'd worry about that tomorrow.

'You've worked hard this week, Dodie. If you're going to relax the regime, you deserve something a lot better than a cheeseburger.'

'I do?' she asked. Then, finding it impossible not to grin, 'I do.'

'Hello, Brad. I was going to call you later. How's it going?'

'The health club is running like clockwork. You've picked a good team, Gina. They're not afraid of responsibility.'

'You've been checking them out? And me?' She didn't wait for his answer, but said, 'And what about Dodie? How's she doing?'

'Better than she thinks. Okay, so there's not much difference in overall size, but what there is—' he found himself needing to take a breath '—is getting thoroughly toned. And she doesn't get out of breath after walking half a mile.' Unlike him, just thinking about how toned she'd looked as they'd walked into Alfredo's last night, in a vivid wrap-around dress that left a deep V between her breasts, with a six-inch-wide contrasting cummerbund emphasising her head-turning, womanly figure.

And heads had turned.

'Progress, indeed,' Gina said, interrupting his chain of thought.

'Well, I've been pretty tough on her. She's only slipped once and I caught her before any damage was done.'

'Well done you.'

He didn't mention that after he'd caught her he'd taken her out to dinner at the most expensive restaurant in town.

That hadn't been about getting her fit. It had been

about getting to know her. Because, no matter how hard he resisted the temptation, he'd finally admitted that he did want to get to know her. Intimately.

They'd spent the evening talking about anything and everything. Films they'd enjoyed. Music. Places they'd visited. Even her glamorous sister.

'How are the wedding plans advancing?' he'd asked her.

'With the precision of a military campaign and the same level of secrecy. I'm not sure that even Natasha knows the date. Now that *Celebrity* magazine is involved, I get the impression that all we have to do is learn our lines and turn up when summoned. And, since the bridesmaid is a non-speaking part...' She shrugged. 'The story of my life, pretty much.'

'You would have liked to be a star? Like your sister?'

'My mother had plans to launch a new theatrical dynasty upon the world. Sadly, I was just not star material. She tried, poor woman. I did the classes, but I was a big disappointment. Two left feet, tone deaf and totally tongue-tied whenever I was asked to perform in public.' She pulled a face. 'Which I suppose, in retrospect, is just as well.'

'You seem to have lost the shyness.' She gave him a quick look. 'You teach...taught.'

'That's easy. I know about that stuff. But ask me to recite a poem to a room full of people...' She shuddered at the memory of it. 'It was a huge relief when Natasha joined the baby dance class and proved a natural. I was able to drop out, retire quietly

to the corner with a box of coloured pencils and a
packet of crisps...'

Something seemed to click in her mind: the connection between being dismissed as worthless and
food, perhaps. She let the sentence hang unfinished,
before lowering her lashes, shrugging again.

'Tell me about you, Brad. Did you always want
to play rugby?'

'Pretty much,' he said, not resisting the change of
subject. She was going to be getting plenty of attention from now on if he had anything to do with it,
once he'd worked out how to break the damaging
cycle of rejection and food. She needed to feel loved
for herself, not because she'd lost a few pounds in
weight. 'University was always going to be less an
opportunity to expand my mind than a chance to
play a lot of rugby.'

'But did you get your degree?'

'Well, yes,' he said, and grinned. 'I didn't go there
to waste my time.'

'And after university?'

'Played for club and country. I was the bright new
star on the horizon.'

'That suggests I should have heard of you.'

'Does it? How interested were you in rugby football at, what...thirteen, fourteen years old?'

'Not very,' she admitted. 'And you were hurt, so
your career didn't last very long. That must have
been a real blow.'

'Life goes on. Worse things happen at sea.' There
wasn't a cliché in the book that he hadn't heard.

But some residue of bitterness must have betrayed

him because she looked up sharply. 'There's something else. It wasn't just your leg, was it?'

It was his turn to shrug. 'Life goes on, Dodie, but when you go from the dizzy heights of being capped for your country to a physical wreck all in one day, not everyone stays aboard for the ride.'

'A girl,' she said. Not a question. 'You were in love with her.'

'Besotted,' he agreed. 'I thought she felt the same way about me. We were engaged to be married, so she should have felt the same way. Apparently it was the fame she was in love with.'

She reached out, covered his hand with her own. 'That's really hard. I'm so sorry.'

And she meant it. She hadn't a clue who or what he was. There was no pretence, no fawning attempt to impress him. She thought he was a guy who'd had a bad break, a guy who wasn't exactly heading for the stars, careerwise. But her big brown eyes were still looking at him as if she'd like to make the pain go away. Make all his dreams come true.

'It's been twelve years,' he said, intending to reassure her. 'There have been a lot of other girls since.'

'But no one to love. Or was it just that you wouldn't allow yourself to take the risk?'

She sounded vaguely wistful, as if she knew from personal experience about never letting anyone that close again, because the hurt might prove fatal. And he discovered that he wanted to wring Martin Jackson's neck for putting her through that.

'I'm over it, Dodie.' And as the warmth of her

fingers seeped through his he realised it was the truth. 'It's time to move on.'

'Brad?' Gina's voice jerked him back to the present. 'Are you still there?'

'Sorry, Gina. I was thinking…'

'About Dodie? Is she there?'

'No, she's in London. An emergency fitting for the dress.'

'Oh, right.'

'I've fixed up a treat for her tomorrow,' he said. 'A surprise. She thinks she's coming in for a morning of serious sweat and strain, but I've booked her in for a salon make-over. Hair, nails, the whole works.'

'Oh, boy. You don't know how much I wish I was there to see all this. I hope you're taking plenty of pictures.'

Pictures of her before. Pictures of her doing a warm-up. Sweating after a workout. On her bike. 'There'll be plenty to choose from,' he said. Then, getting to the real point of his call, 'That's what I wanted to talk to you about. Do we have to do this? Have you actually signed a contract?'

'Sorry?'

'With *Celebrity*? I understand they're covering the wedding. Or was this deal with one of their rivals?'

'I haven't the faintest idea what you're talking about.'

'You didn't arrange for Dodie to use the health club in return for a transformation piece for a magazine? PR?' he prompted, when she didn't reply.

'The wedding? Cinderella sister to Princess bridesmaid courtesy of Lake Spa?'

'I did not.' She said the words carefully and precisely. 'In return for use of the gym, Dodie is going to design and make a textile for that huge blank wall in Reception. That was the ''deal'', and in my judgement it's a good one. No one—' she said, and then said it again, presumably to ram the point home, '*No one* is going to use pictures of Dodie—or anyone else, for that matter—sweating on an exercise machine in my gym. Not for cash. Not even for the PR coup of the century. Not even if it means I have to look for another job. Have I made my feelings plain enough for you?'

More than plain. This was a woman with compassion, integrity, loyalty. He had no more questions to ask about her suitability for promotion. He wanted her on his side.

'You've got another job, Gina,' he said. 'I was going to talk to you about it when you got home, but this seems as good a moment as any to tell you that I want you to take responsibility for the health club division. A directorship and everything that goes with it is yours whenever you want it.'

There was a pause—he hoped it was of the stunned variety—before she said, 'I'll be happy to discuss that with you, Brad. When I've got your word that you won't use those pictures.'

'I was the one who asked you if we had to do it. If we were tied to a contract,' he reminded her, but softly. Then, just to make sure *she'd* got the picture, 'But, just so you have no doubts, you have my word, and although you can't see me I promise you I'm crossing my heart.'

Dodie was supposed to be working, but when he put his head around the door of the studio he found her staring at the pieces she'd assembled for her winter panel. It didn't look much further forward than the last time he'd seen it.

'I thought that was supposed to be finished last week.'

'My personal deadline. Fortunately I've got another couple of weeks before delivery.'

'Then, since you seem to be staring into space, you might as well take a break. I'm about to construct the finest omelette known to man,' he said. 'Want to join me?'

She started, seeming to come out of a distant reverie. 'Thanks, Brad, but I'm not very hungry.'

'You're not working, either.' He walked across to where she was sitting and took her hand. It was freezing, despite a sudden rise in temperature that suggested spring might finally be on its way. 'Come on, leave this,' he said, encouraging her to her feet.

She allowed him to lead her out of the studio and back to the kitchen. 'Tea?' he offered. 'Coffee? A glass of wine?'

'Should you be encouraging me to drink stimulants?'

'You know this isn't punishment, Dodie. You don't have to atone for all the junk food you've ever eaten. You're just making some adjustments to your diet, taking a little exercise so that you can enjoy life more. Not less. You've cycled to the club today, done an hour in the gym, and then you cycled home, despite the fact that I said I'd drive you.'

She smiled absently. 'I looked in the office but you were busy on the phone. Looking like some tycoon fixing up a million-dollar deal.'

'Multi-million,' he teased.

'Oh, pardon me,' she said. 'Some tycoon fixing up a multi-million-dollar deal.'

'You wouldn't believe me if I told you,' he said, grinning.

'No?'

'No,' he said. Out of the blue he'd been offered the chance to buy an abandoned canal basin in the industrial heartland. It was bigger than anything he'd ever done, a huge risk, but there was an opportunity to turn a site of inner city decay into something vibrant, exciting. Housing, offices, conference and leisure facilities. The big challenge he'd needed to get him going. Tear him away from Lake Spa.

Except that nothing was going to tear him away while Dodie needed him.

He didn't say any of that, even though he longed to tell her about it—share his enthusiasm, take her to the site and show her how it was, what it could become.

That was a feeling so new that he didn't quite know how to handle it.

'I'd have put the deal on hold if I'd known you were ready to leave,' he said. And discovered he meant that, too.

'No, it was fine,' she said. 'The ride was good. It's getting warmer. Had you noticed?'

'Yes, I'd noticed. But let up on yourself, okay?'

'It's not the exercise that's getting me down.'

'I saw a letter had come from the University. Have you spoken to Martin James?'

She shook her head, then lifted a shoulder, an awkward gesture that said far more than words. 'I know that the lecture is good for my career. That I'd be mad to turn it down. But I don't want to take anything from him. Not even this.'

'Then tell him so.'

'But—'

'He came to you, Dodie. He wants you. You heard the man. He wants the publicity that goes with your sister's wedding.' Brad forced himself to keep his tone even, non-judgemental. 'He thinks you'll be good for him.'

'I got all that. But he also knows that he'll be good for me. That I can't say no.'

'Then surprise him.'

He reached out to her, pulled her close against his chest, wanting to protect her from everything bad. She didn't resist him any more than she'd resisted his kiss goodnight when they'd got back from the restaurant. But, despite the temptation to take it further, he kept it light. She had demons and, much as he wanted to slay them for her, she had to face this one herself before she could move on. Not that he was going to leave it entirely to her.

'There'll be other opportunities. Let this one go.'

She looked up. 'You think?'

'I know. Just do it so that he knows you're not still licking your wounds. That you're the one in control.'

'That'll be a first.'

'Trust me. Call him first thing tomorrow, ask him to meet you for lunch at the health club.' She raised her eyebrows, surprised. 'You'll have the advantage of home territory, a place where everyone knows your name.'

'Suppose he doesn't want to come?'

'Don't give him a chance to say no. Just tell him when and where, and if he tries to prolong the conversation say you're busy and hang up.' He grinned. 'You will be. I'll see to that.'

'Not the treadmill,' she begged, and he was pleased to see that she could laugh, even with this hanging over her. 'Please, guv, not the treadmill.'

'No, I promise you it won't be that. I've got something else lined up for tomorrow morning.'

'That sounds ominous,' she said, but didn't press it. 'Okay, Mr Wise Guy. I get him to the restaurant. What then?'

'Tell him that you'd love to do the lecture under any other circumstances. Unfortunately you have to turn it down for personal reasons. You don't have to spell them out—he'll get the picture.'

'Well, that's very…ladylike.'

'You are a lady.'

'Even so, I can't see him just giving up.'

'You just keep repeating that you'd love to do it, but that you have to turn it down—'

'—because of personal reasons.' A tiny, hopeful

little smile lifted the corners of her mouth. 'It's that self-assertiveness stuff, isn't it?'

'That's right. You listen to what he has to say, then you repeat your piece, and you keep doing that until he hears you.'

'It sounds easy.' She still sounded doubtful.

'Piece of cake,' he said, and with one arm still around her he picked up a bottle of wine that was already open on the table, scooping up the glasses with his long fingers. 'Come on. I lit a fire in the sitting room. Let's go and drink this in comfort.'

'What about your supper? The omelette?'

'It'll keep,' he said, backing her onto a sofa that had been neatly covered in cream calico to reflect the simple décor. He poured the wine. 'Drink this. It'll give you courage. Warm the cockles of your heart.'

She took the glass, looking up at him, the firelight reflected in her eyes. 'Why are you so good to me?'

'Because it pleases me,' he said. 'Because I think you're very special.' And then, his voice catching on the words, 'Just because.'

'I...I don't know what to say.'

'Say nothing. Drink your wine; enjoy the fire.'

He put down his glass and settled beside her, lifting his arm in a wordless invitation to snuggle up, and she came to him, settling against his chest as if it was the most natural thing in the world.

'What was her name?' she said, after a moment.

He didn't ask who she was talking about. Didn't have to. Any more than she had to say. He didn't pretend to have forgotten, either.

'Lisa,' he said. 'Blue eyes, corn-blonde hair. She looked like an angel. Unfortunately she had all the character of a plastic one you'd put on top of your Christmas tree.'

She relaxed. 'Thank you.'

'You're welcome.'

That she cared, that she'd been thinking about it, that it was important enough to ask, told him everything he wanted to know.

And it also gave him the opening he needed.

'Now it's my turn.' She lifted her head to look up at him. 'To ask a question.'

'You want me to tell you about Martin. What he did.'

Actually, it didn't take a lot of imagination. It was the telling that was more important than the listening. 'Get rid of it, Dodie. Don't keep it locked up inside to seep poison into your soul.'

'That degree you were swanning through while you worked at becoming a sports legend—it wouldn't have been in psychology, by any chance?'

'The word sounds vaguely familiar. It's got to be fifteen years ago, but I seem to recall my tutor saying that I was psychologically unfit for anything more demanding than kicking a ball between two posts. Something he couldn't see any point in.' He glanced down at her. 'Of course the man had no *heol*.'

'*Heol?*'

'It's a Welsh word. And untranslatable. It comes closest to heart, I suppose.' And he briefly laid his fist against his own heart. 'But it's more than that. Bigger. It's everything you feel about something you love. When your heart is bursting with it. For your home. Your country.' A woman for whom you'd lay down your life.

'Rugby football?' she asked, a hint of teasing in her voice.

'On the day of an international, wearing a shirt in your country's colours with a hundred thousand voices singing the national anthem? Oh, yes.'

She kicked off her shoes and curled her legs beneath her, sipped her wine. 'It's a beautiful word.'

'Tell me, Dodie,' he insisted, refusing to let her slip away from dealing with Martin Jackson.

She looked up at him. 'You don't need me to tell you. You know what he did, Brad. He cheated on me.'

Surprise, surprise. 'Tell me.'

'Are you trying that assertiveness stuff on me?'

'Tell me,' he said.

She turned and looked into the flames flickering around the logs in the hearth, and it was a while before she spoke, taking her time to sort through memory.

'Martin had been to London. He had some pictures to sell. One of those bright young artists he'd spotted had made a splash in the news for doing something totally off the wall and he was cashing in while it lasted. He took up some other work to be looked at by a gallery he did business with. He was good at promoting the students he thought were special.'

'The students whose work he'd bought. Giving

them a helping hand into the limelight so that his investment wasn't wasted.'

'It's obvious when you think about it. I guess I wasn't thinking.' She took another sip of wine, her hand shaking a little. 'My last class of the day was cancelled. Part of the ceiling in my department had collapsed after a heavy rainstorm. It's an old building and the roof needs attention. I could have stayed on and done some catch-up on paperwork, but I decided to go home early and cook something special for dinner. I didn't expect him to be here. He didn't hear me let myself in.'

It had happened here? In her home? He hadn't counted on that. And yet it explained the clear-out.

'Dodie—'

'You can't hear the kitchen door open from in here,' she said, then frowned. 'I couldn't, for a moment, think what was happening…but then I came through and saw for myself.'

'Dodie, I'm sorry. There's no need to go on—'

But it was as if he'd wound up a clockwork toy, and nothing would stop it until it had finished what he'd set in motion.

'He hadn't been back long—hadn't done more than unbutton his overcoat. He was sitting on the sofa, his head thrown back, eyes closed, and one of those students who so adored him for helping them get noticed was on her knees…''thanking'' him…'

'He was with a student?'

'I know. Bad form. But it happens. She begged me not to tell. Swore it was her fault. That he'd called her on the way home, told her that he'd sold one of her pictures. She'd just wanted to show her gratitude…'

'He was in a position of trust. He should have known better.'

'She wasn't a child, Brad. She was twenty-one. His actions might have been morally ambiguous but she knew what she was doing. And, frankly, I wasn't particularly eager to tell anyone what had happened.'

Except Gina, he thought. Loyal, compassionate and fiercely protective of her friend.

'So you kept silent and left a job you loved?'

'It seems silly, I expect. I'd thrown him out of my house. Scrubbed it from top to bottom. Thrown out every piece of bedlinen, every towel…'

She made an unconscious gesture, rubbing at her sleeve, and he knew she'd scrubbed herself as well. It took every ounce of self-control not to simply sweep her into his arms, hold her, tell her everything in his heart.

She wasn't ready to hear that. Not yet.

'Re-upholstered the sofa?' he prompted.

'The sofa?' She looked puzzled. 'Oh, no. I sold that. This was pretty tatty, but at least I could live with it.' She sighed. 'I thought if I cleaned him out of my life,' she said, 'I could cope. But every time I looked at a student all I could see was that girl and what she'd been doing to Martin. Asking myself if she was the only one. Knowing in my heart that she wasn't. Wondering which of those pretty young girls—handsome young men—looking up at me had been…grateful.'

'Tomorrow he'll wish he'd been kinder. You'll be

able to look him in the eye and see that he was a fool. And he'll see it too. Then you'll be free of him.'

He unwound his arm and got to his feet while he still had the will-power to move. 'Now,' he said, taking her hand, pulling her up alongside him, 'let's cook. You beat and I'll chop—'

He opened the fridge door—closed it again. 'What happened to your photograph?'

She shrugged. 'It's fallen off, I expect. It'll have joined all the other notes that have slipped under the fridge. I'll print another one tomorrow.'

CHAPTER NINE

'YOUR lunch date's arrived, Dodie,' one of the receptionists said, putting her head around the office door. 'And your one o'clock appointment is here, Brad.'

Dodie, her hair done, her make-up perfect and her fingers polished a dark and sexy red, nevertheless started involuntarily.

'I'll be right there—' she began.

Brad reached out, took her hand, stopped her from going anywhere.

'Take Mr Jackson up to the bar, Lucy, give him a drink and the menu. Tell him Dodie knows he's here and will be along in a minute.'

When the receptionist had gone, he said, 'Make him wait. You're in control, remember?'

'I'm also shaking like a leaf. I'm throwing away the chance of a lifetime.'

'There'll be other chances.'

'Maybe. But it's not just that. I'm not used to saying what I want…making people listen to me.'

'Then you're going to enjoy yourself today.' He cocked a brow. 'Say it.'

'I'm going to enjoy myself today?'

He grinned. 'I was hoping for a little more conviction.'

'For acting you need my sister.'

'You'll do just fine.' He continued to hold her hand. 'You look wonderful, Dodie.'

She glanced down at herself. The black linen coat-dress no longer gaped unattractively over her bust, but she would hardly describe her appearance as 'wonderful'.

'I suppose two dress sizes was a bit ambitious.'

'I like you just the way you are.'

He lifted her chin, making her look up at him. He looked pretty wonderful, too. Dressed to kill in a cream suit, dark blue shirt.

'You look wonderful,' he repeated, stroking his thumb along her jaw. 'You are beautiful.'

She knew he was saying it to bolster her confidence, so she resisted the natural urge to say, *Rubbish*. He had been unbelievably kind. And last night he'd been a perfect gentleman. Unfortunately.

She had the feeling that she was always going to regret not going for it when he'd been ready and willing...

But...

But after today it would be over. Gina would be home and Brad would be moving on. Job done. She didn't need him any more. Not as a prop, anyway. There had been no dramatic weight loss but she was trimmer, fitter. Self-respect back in place. Those were the things she'd wanted.

And if she'd discovered rather too late that the one thing she really, really wanted was Brad Morgan...well, she would have to live with it. She certainly wouldn't be stockpiling the chocolate and crying into her pillow. Life was too short for that.

Instead she looked up at him, smiled. 'If I am, it's thanks to you, Brad.'

'Highlights, a manicure, a make-up job. They're nothing. Just gilding on the lily. You are equally lovely when you're wearing a baggy jog-suit. Even first thing in the morning without a scrap of make-up and wearing PJs that would embarrass a two-year-old.' He grinned. 'Of course on you they're the sexiest things I've ever seen.'

He was bolstering her confidence; of course he was. She recognised that even as the colour seeped into her face, as hope made her heart beat just a little faster.

'Those rabbits…' he said.

The flush deepened.

'Even pink in the face and out of breath.'

He touched a cheek with cool knuckles.

She was still shaking, but not with fear. 'It was definitely psychology,' she said, her voice slightly ragged.

'You think?' He shrugged. 'Would a psychologist kiss his patient?'

'I don't know,' she admitted. Then, 'Are you going to kiss me?'

In answer, he touched his lips very gently to hers. 'Mustn't spoil the make-up,' he said, looking down at her.

She was tempted to say that she could redo her lipstick in a second. Better not.

'No,' she said. 'Of course not.' Especially when it was so clearly a goodbye kiss.

'Okay, he's waited long enough. Go and tell

Jackson that he's got nothing you want.' For the briefest moment he held her. 'Go. I have to show an important new member around the club.'

Martin looked up as she walked across the bar and his eyebrows rose a fraction as he took in her appearance. A satisfied smirk marred his handsome face. He thought she'd made an effort to impress him, she realised. He thought he'd got her at his feet.

That smirk made it very easy to wait for him to stand up, pull back a chair for her. It took him a moment to catch on, but he finally got the message.

'I scarcely recognised you, Dodie. You've done something to your hair. Lost a bit of weight. You look surprisingly good.'

Patronising oaf.

'Still water. No ice,' she said. He seemed at something of a loss. 'Didn't you ask me what I wanted to drink?' She'd seen Natasha do that in a film. It was amazingly effective. He actually flushed.

How on earth could she have been taken in by this man?

As if in answer, a passing waitress stopped midstride as he glanced in her direction, raised a hand. That was how. He just used those dark, come-to-bed eyes and women responded mindlessly. He ordered her drink, and another for himself, then looked around.

'This is nice. I'm not much of a man for physical jerks, but this kind of place attracts people with real money. I think I'll apply for membership.'

'I'll ask Gina to put a form in the post, shall I?'

'Gina?'

'She's the manager here. Unfortunately she's in Los Angeles on business at the moment. I know how sorry she'll be to have missed giving you her answer in person.'

He laughed, but not with much humour. 'Maybe I won't bother.'

'Waste of a stamp, I would have thought,' she agreed.

'You're not going to be difficult about this, are you, Dodie? I know you're angry with me, but it's been nearly a year. You can see how I'm trying to make it up to you. The Armstrong Lecture…'

'I know. It'll be good for my career. Nevertheless, I'm going to have to decline the invitation.'

He laughed, unconvinced. 'Okay, fair enough. I can understand your need to make me sweat a bit, but I've already told the Vice Chancellor that you'll do it, Dodie. He's very excited about the publicity.'

'I do hope you didn't tell him that my sister would come to hear me speak, because he's going to be doubly disappointed.'

His smile faded as he realised she was serious. 'It would be so much more pleasant if you just agreed.'

That sounded ominously like a threat, but the minute she'd set eyes on him all her trepidation had fallen away. This man had taken away what little self-respect she'd had. Some time in the last few weeks—with Brad Morgan's help—she'd rediscovered it.

'We both know it's your career you're worrying about, not mine.' She smiled her thanks at the waitress. A waste of time. The woman only had eyes for Martin. She sympathised; she'd been there. But not any more. 'My mind is made up, Martin.'

'Perhaps this will unmake it for you.' She'd been aware of the large brown envelope that lay on the table between them. Now he picked it up and handed it to her.

'What is it?' she asked. 'A personal note from the Vice Chancellor?'

'It's a little incentive to be a good girl, Dodie.'

'I resigned as your doormat a year ago,' she said, but without any hint of bitterness—he didn't matter enough for bitterness—as she lifted the flap. Inside was a photograph. The one Brad had taken of her, red-faced, out of breath and looking as if she was about to expire. The picture that, until yesterday, had been fixed to her fridge door.

She remembered the way Martin had looked at it.

'You've been in my home? You kept a key?'

'One never knows when such a thing will be useful,' he said, without apology. 'Have you any idea how much the tabloids would pay for a picture of Natasha's big sister getting in shape for the wedding?' he asked.

She knew. Photographers had been camped outside her mother's house for two weeks on the off-chance that Natasha would visit. There were some advantages to being the invisible member of the family.

'No, but I'm sure you do, Martin.' She resisted the temptation to tear the photograph into shreds—he'd undoubtedly anticipated such a reaction and

had made copies—and instead returned it to him as
she got to her feet. 'However, my answer is still no.
And lunch is cancelled. I'm sure you can find your
own way out.'

She turned her back on him, the only thing in her
mind getting her locks changed. Brad, deep in conversation with a tall, elegant woman of about his
own age, was heading towards them. The important
new member he was showing around the health
club? A new client? Someone with the money to pay
his expensive hourly fee...

In her head she'd known that he wasn't going to
be around for ever. He was an expensive luxury and
she'd had him just for a little while. On loan.

Her heart had apparently been hoping he might
choose to stay.

Stupid. If he'd been going to stay he wouldn't
have kissed her cheek last night and left her at her
bedroom door.

Even as the thoughts raced through her head
Brad's companion detached herself from him and
came towards her, her hand extended.

'Miss Layton, what a pleasure to meet you. Brad
has just been telling me that you've been commissioned to do a hanging for the health club—'

She glanced at him. He knew that? His expression
remained totally neutral.

'—and when he said you were having lunch here
today I begged him to introduce me.'

'Dodie, I'd like you meet Willow Armstrong,'
Brad said, stepping in to perform the introductions.
'She runs the Armstrong Media Group. Her husband

is Mike Armstrong—the furniture designer,' he added, as if she didn't know. 'The man who instigated the annual Armstrong Lectures.'

'We were lucky enough to have Brad as one of our first speakers,' Willow said. 'On the importance of sport in schools.' She smiled up at him. 'He's credited with saving a lot of playing fields from the developers. At some personal cost.'

'Oh?' Dodie said, finally finding her voice.

'When the High School playing field was put on the market he bought it at development rates and then put it into trust so that no one else could build on it,' Willow explained.

Something caught in Dodie's throat, and for a moment she couldn't speak, couldn't even look at him. 'I didn't know that,' she said. There was a lot she didn't know, apparently. Even Gina had kept this secret.

'I really love your work, Miss Layton—'

'What? Oh, Dodie, please.'

'Dodie,' she repeated. 'I have a piece of yours called *Dandelion Clock*. It's stunning.' She turned to Brad. 'It's an explosion of dandelion seed heads...whites and creams and the subtlest colours. Layer after layer. I see something new every time I look at it.'

'Thank you.'

'Brad tells me that you're going to turn down our invitation to give a lecture this year. I understand the pressure of work, but I hoped if I asked you personally I might persuade you to change your mind.'

'Why don't you and Willow have lunch?' Brad

cut in smoothly, before Dodie could demand answers to any of the million questions that were bubbling up inside her head. 'Talk it over.' Then, 'Martin—don't you have to be somewhere else? Let me walk you to the door.'

She found Brad in Gina's office. Or was that *his* office? Since it was evident from some of the things Willow had said that he owned everything around here. And a lot more.

He was standing at the window, looking out over the lake, apparently waiting for her.

'Sorted?' he said, without looking around.

'Sorted,' she confirmed, her insides a jumble of confused emotions. She was seething with anger. Furious with him. Wanted to throttle him for *pretending*, making a total fool of her. So why did she want to throw her arms around him and hug him to death? 'But then, since you clearly stage-managed the whole thing, you already know that,' she said, settling for the dangerous calm that had gripped her. He neither confirmed nor denied it. 'I mean Willow Armstrong didn't turn up here today by accident, did she?'

'No, it wasn't an accident.' He looked back at her, lifted his shoulders in the merest shrug. 'I could have by-passed Martin Jackson, but I thought you needed to look him in the eye and tell him face-to-face to get lost.'

'Well, I did,' she said, struggling with her breathing. Then, abruptly, 'Thank you.'

'Don't thank me, Dodie. You did it. I'm just sorry

that you couldn't see his face while Willow was begging you to reconsider.' And he sketched one of his telling little smiles. This one told her that he thought he deserved the benefit of the doubt.

Damn, damn, damn! How could she stay angry with him when he did that? When her own mouth responded without any help from her brain? 'What did you say to him?' she asked. 'As you walked him to the door?'

'Just advised him to explore other career opportunities. I may not be as ''busy'' as Martin Jackson—I do, however, have a lot of friends in high places.' Then, 'Would you like to take a walk?' he invited, indicating the sunny deck beyond the open window.

She swallowed, certain that this was going to be goodbye.

'Do I have to do stretches first?' she asked.

'It's entirely up to you,' he said, regarding her bosom with more than passing interest. 'Will those buttons stand the strain?'

'Not a chance.'

'Then, please, go ahead.'

She looked up at him. Saw something in his expression that made her blush. She let him take her hand, lead her out onto the deck. 'I'm afraid Martin may yet have the last laugh,' she said—because she had to say something and it couldn't be what she was feeling—and told him about the photograph.

He winced. 'Gina will kill me. I gave her my word that none of the photographs would be published.' He glanced at her. 'Can you handle it?'

'It might have hurt if I'd still looked like that. Now it'll just raise interest in me. In my work. And it's got a lovely view of the health club in the background. Nice PR for Gina.' Then, after a careful breath, 'And of course for you.'

'Unfortunately that just makes it worse. She'll think it was planned.' And he told her about the misunderstanding.

'You thought all those photographs were going to be used for publicity?' she demanded. 'Well, thanks.'

'If it's any consolation I'd much rather have an original Dodie Layton than any amount of publicity.'

That explained why he'd given her so much attention. Withdrawing her hand from his, she said, 'You needn't worry. I'll tell Gina what happened.' There was a seat at the end of the deck and she sat down, glanced up at him. 'If you'll explain why no one around here treats you like a multi-millionaire entrepreneur…?'

'Maybe because I don't act like one?' he offered, joining her, sliding his arm along the back of the seat.

That was true, at least, she thought, trying to ignore the way his fingers brushed against her neck. Brad Morgan owned everything as far as she could see. Controlled a leisure empire that was worth more millions than she could count. But for the last three weeks he'd slept in her spare bedroom. Cooking. Doing the washing up. Sharing the chores.

Giving her back her life. Her self-confidence. Her pride.

For a bit of PR? How likely was that?

'Do you regularly take time out to play personal trainer?' she enquired.

'No, you're a one-off, Dodie. And I won't be doing it again.'

'It was that bad, huh?'

'Well, the plumbing was different.'

'Oh…' She groaned as she remembered the way she'd asked him to change the washers on her taps. 'Oh, no. I thought you were… I asked you to…'

He retrieved her hand, held it tight. 'Did I let you down?'

'No. You did a great job. I told Gina…' She let her head fall into her lap, shaking it. There was no way she was going to tell him what she'd told Gina. 'She never said a word.'

She didn't ask why. She knew why. Gina had been playing Cupid, big time, and her arrow had hit the mark.

'Why didn't you tell me?' she asked, shivering a little as a chill came off the water. He slipped off his jacket, put it around her shoulders, keeping his arm there.

'I've been asking myself that since last night. Ever since I realised that I'd painted myself into a corner.' A duck, spotting them, cruised up to the edge of the deck looking for food. 'It didn't seem to matter at first. You were just a woman who needed a one-on-one personal trainer.'

She remembered how she'd felt. Desperate to look good for the wedding. For Charles Gray. For anything but herself.

How long ago that seemed.

'And in return you thought there was going to be a big PR pay-off?'

'I didn't move in with you because of that, Dodie. When Gina told me that you'd wanted her to move in with you I leapt at the chance. You turned me on like the National Grid. That night with the chocolate you thought I was just being kind. You were wrong. I've never wanted a woman more.'

'But that was before…'

'Before you lost weight, got toned, had highlights? Absolutely.'

'I wish I'd known. I wanted you so much, Brad. After you'd gone I nearly passed out with sheer longing.'

'Yeah, well, believe me, you weren't on your own. But you were so vulnerable. I wanted to hold you, just hold you and tell you how much I wanted you, but you would never have believed me. I wanted you to believe me so much. And I needed to know that you cared for me the way I was beginning to care for you. The way I do care for you.'

'You needed to know that I wasn't flinging myself at you at every opportunity just for the glamour. Or the money. Is that what all those other girls have done?'

'That was their main appeal,' he said gently, holding her close. 'There's more than one way of being vulnerable, but I knew I'd never lose my heart to a gold-digger.'

'Oh.'

'Then, last night, I realised that I'd have to tell you the truth and that you'd think I'd lied to you.'

'You didn't exactly lie. I leapt to conclusions; you didn't correct them.'

He looked down at her. 'Now you're being kind.'

'Okay,' she said, 'you were economical with the truth. But not with any intention of hurting me.'

'No. That was the last thing I wanted to do. You needed someone, Dodie, and I elected myself. But I don't think you'd have been very comfortable with Gina's boss moving into your spare room.'

'No.' She glanced at him sideways, from beneath her lashes, her heart beating uncomfortably fast as she said, 'I don't imagine you were very comfortable in that narrow little bed, either.'

'I had sleepless nights,' he admitted. 'But it had nothing to do with the bed. Everything to do with the woman sleeping on the other side of the landing.'

'Last night—'

'Last night was too soon.'

'Too soon?'

'You recognised that when I lost it over the chocolate. You nearly lost it over the cheeseburger, but we both had baggage that needed to be jettisoned. Bitterness on my part. Martin Jackson on yours.'

'Plus twenty pounds excess weight,' she added.

'You haven't lost twenty pounds.' He moved his arm to her waist, pulled her close. 'You're never going to be skinny,' he said, his mouth nuzzling her ear. 'But you know something?'

Since he was now breathing a trail of moist kisses along the line of her jaw, heading in the direction of her mouth, she couldn't quite find the breath to ask him what.

'I love you just the way you are.'

She pulled back, looked up into his eyes. He'd said that once before. Only then he'd said 'like'.

For a moment it felt as if the world had stopped. Then the corner of his mouth lifted in a smile that said...*I meant that*. And deepened into...*I really meant that*. And then changed to something that she could have sworn said...*Can we continue this conversation somewhere more private, where I can get your clothes off and show you exactly how I feel?*

'Now?' she said, answering his unasked question.

'Now,' he agreed. 'Let's go home—'

'There you are!' Dodie flinched at the sound of her mother's voice. 'I've been ringing you all morning. Why do you bother to carry a cellphone if you don't switch it on? Don't listen to your messages?' She came to halt in front of them. 'Well, thank goodness you've had your hair fixed. It looks almost as good as Natasha's, although of course she has hers cut personally by...' She let it go. 'Come along. We haven't got much time.'

'Time? Time for what?'

Her mother responded with a significant jerk of her head in Brad's direction. *The wedding,* she mouthed silently. Then, 'It's this evening. We're dodging the...you know...'

'The paparazzi?' Dodie offered.

Dorothy Layton threw up her hands in a gesture of despair. 'For goodness' sake. Tell the whole world, why don't you?'

'Just Brad. Mother, this is Brad Morgan. Brad, my mother, Dorothy Layton.'

He leaned forward to offer his hand, but kept his other arm firmly about her waist as if to warn her that she wasn't going anywhere without him. 'How d'you do, Mrs Layton?'

'How d'you do?' she replied, barely giving him a glance. 'Darling, we have to go.'

'Brad's coming to the wedding, Mother.'

'Really, Dodie! You can't just bring extra people at the last moment. I'm sorry Mr…'

'Gina's not back from America. He's…um…deputising for her.' Then, suddenly nervous, she glanced at him. Maybe he wouldn't want to come…

'Dodie and I have unfinished business, Mrs Layton. You take her, I'm afraid you get me.'

For a moment she looked as if she was about to argue. Then, 'Whatever,' she said, as if beyond caring. 'The ceremony's taking place at Melchester Castle at 6 o'clock,' she told them. 'You'll need to be there in plenty of time to get into your dress, make-up, whatever. I don't want you spoiling your sister's big day, so don't be late.'

'Don't worry about spoiling *my* big day,' Dodie muttered, as her mother rushed off.

'It's a long way from over,' Brad said, flipping open a mobile phone as she glanced at him. 'I meant that about unfinished business. Just wait for the word.'

'What word?'

He said nothing, just smiled. And this smile was unreadable.

'We'd better go home and pick up some stuff.' He tossed her the keys to his 4 x 4. 'You drive while I break the habit of lifetime and act like a millionaire. I'll get us a suite at the Melchester Castle Hotel,' he said, calling up a number. 'And a more suitable form of transport. We've both been very, very good. I think we deserve a treat.'

Melchester Castle was a picturesque ruin much loved by nineteenth-century watercolour painters. It had been abandoned centuries earlier in favour of the more comfortable surroundings of a Tudor manor, now an equally picturesque hotel.

They circled it from the air before the pilot set the helicopter down.

Hotel servants rushed out to take their baggage, seemingly confused by the fact that they only had a suit carrier and an overnight bag between them.

'We thought you were Miss Layton arriving,' one the lads said.

'I am Miss Layton,' Dodie said. Well, she was the older sister. The distinction was hers. 'Natasha Layton is my little sister.'

Her mother was waiting in Reception, dressed in a pale blue silk two-piece and a hat large enough to shade a border. 'Oh, it's just you, Dodie. I thought I heard a helicopter.'

'I'm beginning to feel the urgent need for a cheeseburger,' Dodie murmured through gritted teeth as she was steered towards the stairs to change.

Then, as Brad looked up from the reception desk where he was signing the register, she grinned, 'But I'll hold out for something better.'

The ceremony was simple, despite the theatrical backdrop of the ruined castle. There were no small bridesmaids or pageboys to cause mayhem. Or other bridesmaids to steal Dodie's limelight.

The bride was heart-stoppingly lovely. The groom, apparently stunned at his good fortune, said 'I do' with total sincerity. Charles Gray, as good-looking as his screen presence suggested, produced the ring without a hitch, and afterwards at the reception made a short but witty speech, toasting the lovely bridesmaid with engaging charm, looking at her as if she were one of his lovely leading ladies and this was their close-up. Maybe he'd been rehearsing the moment for weeks, but it didn't show.

The bride and groom took centre stage and danced slowly around the room to the applause of the onlookers. Then Charles Gray asked Dodie if she'd like to join them.

This was it. Dream come true time. And all she wanted was to dance with Brad. Her hand resting lightly in his. His possessively at her waist. But he'd been recognised by some rugby fanatic and was now surrounded by half a dozen men—one of them her father—who were apparently reliving a ball-by-ball replay of the latest international. He caught her eye, smiled.

Ah. It was deliberate, then. This was what she'd

wanted and he was standing back, giving her centre stage for her starring role.

Well, if you had to take second best Charles Gray was as good as it got, she supposed, and she allowed him to lead her onto the floor. He danced as perfectly as he did everything else, turning at just the right moment to smile into the waiting cameras. They had only made it halfway around the dance floor before Brad cut in.

'Now,' he said, with that unreadable smile as he held out his hand.

'That's a good word,' she said, taking it.

Charles Gray looked as if he'd never been abandoned on a dance floor—or anywhere else—before. But he took it in good part, smiling broadly as he bent to kiss her cheek—a photograph that was destined to feature in *Celebrity*—and told Brad that he was a lucky man. Something he assured the actor that he already knew.

'Dodie…' Her mother waylaid them. 'Your sister's just going up to change.'

'She doesn't need me. She's got a husband to help her with her buttons…' But the staircase was blocked. Her sister was at the top of the stairs, ready to toss her bouquet.

'Let's take the lift,' Dodie said, but before they could escape Natasha spotted her, called out her name.

'Dodie! Catch!' And she turned and tossed the bouquet over her shoulder.

It would have sailed clear over her head, but Brad put up his hand and plucked it out of the air. All eyes swivelled in his direction and for a moment there was an expectant hush, then he turned to her and, as he offered her the bouquet, said, 'Would you consider starring in a sequel, Miss Layton?'

'A sequel?'

A voice from the crowd shouted helpfully, *'Miss Layton Gets Married Two.'*

Everyone laughed, but she didn't hear them. He was asking her to marry him?

He couldn't be... It was impossible. And yet she was the centre of attention, with dozens of people hanging on her answer.

But the only person who mattered at that moment was standing right in front of her, and for once in his life Brad Morgan wasn't smiling. There wasn't even the tiniest tuck in the corner of his mouth to betray what he was thinking.

In fact he was absolutely, totally serious, she realised.

'But I don't want to be a star,' she said. 'Equal billing suits me just fine.'

'It's yours, Dodie. Anything you want.'

'I've got everything I want,' she said, reaching out to accept the bouquet from him before flinging her arms around his neck and kissing him as a deep, collective sigh erupted from every corner of the room.

He drew back a little, looked down at her. 'Same time, same place?' he murmured. 'As soon as you like?'

'Yes,' she said. 'Please.' Then, as they turned and realised everyone was looking at them, 'Brad?'

'Yes, sweetheart?'

'Now!'

Without hesitation he bent and caught her behind the knees, and the crowd fell back, applauding as he carried her up the stairs.

It was a still June day, the sun shining as once again the Layton family and their friends were gathered in the ruins of the Melchester Castle.

Dodie passed her bouquet to Gina. Gina was so busy exchanging meaningful glances with the best man that she nearly dropped it.

The best man, a rugby international who'd survived his sport without sustaining anything worse than a broken nose, had to be prompted twice to produce the ring.

And even if the press weren't hanging out of the trees to take photographs of them exchanging their vows—the way they had at her sister's wedding—when Brad slipped the ring on her finger and, looking into her eyes, said the old, sweet words... 'With this ring I thee wed...' it was still the biggest day in Dodie's life

So far.

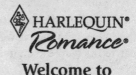

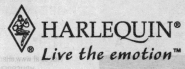

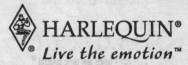

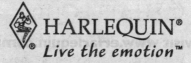